SISTER MARGARET

SISTER MARGARET

A Tommy Keane Novel

**Travis Myers &
Natasha Myers Marsiguerra**

Sister Margaret is a work of fiction. Names, characters, and incidents are the product of the author's imagination and are used fictitiously. Any resemblance to actual events, or persons, living or dead, is entirely coincidental.

Published in the United States by Bully Press Corp.

Bully Press Corp
P. O. Box 404
Wingdale, NY 12594 United States

Cover design by: Phred Rawles

ISBN-13: 978-1-7343370-0-6

For our mother, Mary.

Thanks for giving us our love of literature.

***

Dedicated to every Cop and Detective, in every city, in every country on the planet. Thank you for standing on the side of right, and for fighting the good and never-ending fight against those who would destroy all we hold dear.

Big thanks to our spouses, Christine and Peter, for putting up with us and all the nonsense we get into. We know it's not always easy.

Big thanks also to Seth Dellon for pointing us in the right direction with this book just when we needed it. You rock, kid.

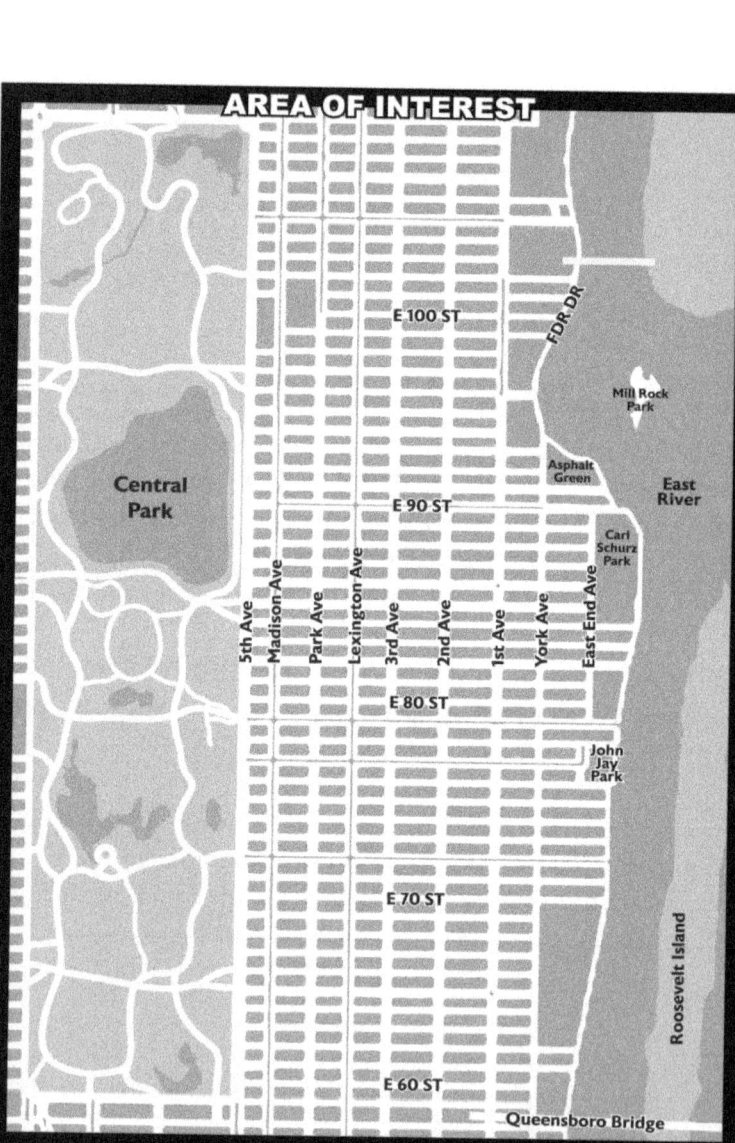

"A man you don't meet every day. Yeah... Tommy's the kinda guy you don't meet every day. Not these days anyway. He's the sorta fella that always tries to do the right thing, keeps his thoughts and words to himself unless it's something that really needs sayin'."

~Bartender, Jack Norris

Prologue ~ Summer

It was a hot and muggy summer day in the Bronx. People sat on their stoops, in tank tops, drinking beer while kids tried to find some relief from the sweltering heat in the flowing water of the open fire hydrants. It was also the day that Sammy Melendez, a fifty year-old building superintendent, brutally murdered one Leon Little in the hallway of the building they both lived in on 198th Street.

Leon was a career criminal. He had been in and out of jail and rehab for twenty-five of his thirty-six years. Sammy, on the other hand, was a hard working super who took pride in keeping his building clean and safe.

Leon Little had spent this particular morning getting high on crack and decided to practice using the samurai sword he had stolen from beneath his younger brother's bed. He swung it around the bedroom, felt its weight, and liked the power he imagined it gave him. Leon took the sword with him out into the rear courtyard of the building, where he spied the two dogs Mr. Melendez kept as a deterrent to burglars, drug dealers, and other miscreants likely to prey on his building and its inhabitants.

Leon, entering a cocaine-fueled psychosis, badly wanted to test the mettle of his newly found blade, and so he descended on the dogs who sat panting in the shade of the hot courtyard. He approached the first one, a large black pit bull named Shadow, who was barking at Leon and straining against his chain. With the first swing of the sword Leon nearly decapitated the dog, which excited him even more. His altered mind immediately sprung into a frenzy.

Leon started to cackle and swing the sword around until he was out of breath. He leaned over with his hands on his knees and surveyed what he had done, impressed by his own strength. He let out another delighted cackle, and then brought the blade down upon the second beast--a white and brown pit bull named Charming. He struck hard, severing the dog's spine and then, with a second swing, cleaved his head almost in half.

Leon then stood up straight and gazed upon the pieces of the two dogs that were scattered on the warm concrete in a growing pool of blood. The flowers and bushes that Sammy Melendez had lovingly maintained were splattered with red. Leon smiled, turned around, and went back inside.

When Sammy Melendez came out of his building to check on his two cherished dogs, animals he had raised and nurtured since birth, he found them hacked into pieces and let out a wail of shock and anguish. In desperation, he turned around in circles unsure of what to do. He spotted blood drops and dark red footprints leading into the building and he followed the trail up to the second floor, straight to Leon Little's auntie's apartment. In a rage, Sammy raced back down the stairs to his basement apartment and armed himself.

He grabbed the cut-down baseball bat that he kept in a chipped umbrella stand by the front door, as well as an eight-inch military-style knife from the drawer in the TV stand. Full of fury, and now with tears running down his face, Sammy returned to the door on the second floor and struck it firmly and repeatedly with the bottom of the knife, which was grasped tightly in his left hand.

"What da fuck you bangin' about nigga," Leon said in a loud and agitated voice as he flung the door open.

Sammy, seeing the blood stains drying on Leon's dingy wife beater, shot his left hand out, like a boxer's jab, straight into Leon's mouth, with all eight inches of the knife going straight through and out the back of Leon's neck. Leon fell onto the dirty linoleum and Sammy pounded his head with the baseball bat, crushing the top and side of Leon's skull.

***

Detective Tommy Keane from the 5-3 Detective Squad and his partner, Samuel Isaacs, were called to the building. After surveilling the crime scene and talking with the uniforms they decided to start their interviews with the building's superintendent. They entered the building and took the stairs down to the basement, pleasantly surprised at how clean and urine-free the stairwell was. They knocked on the super's door and when Sammy Melendez opened it and saw the two detectives standing there, he immediately confessed.

"It was me! I did it," he blurted out. "But come. Come look what he did to my fuckin dogs."

Keane and Isaacs stood in disbelief at the site of the two dogs that lay mutilated in the courtyard surrounded by a dark puddle of blood.

"Motherfucker," Isaacs mumbled to himself. They took Mr. Melendez into custody, recovered all of the weapons, took statements from the neighbors and Leon's aunt, and went about the long and arduous task of booking Sammy and vouchering the evidence. Neither detective knew Sammy personally, but after spending the better part of nine hours in his company, they decided he was a good and decent man.

He was one of the Bronx's hardworking people who took care of his family and community. Unfortunately, on this day, he had acted out of passion, and would have to pay the consequences.

"If Leon wasn't home," Tommy said to Isaacs, "Had there been even a couple hours in between the discovery of the dogs and the meeting on the 2nd floor, this would have never happened."

"Yeah, well it is what it is. Fucking tragedy. This Melendez seems like a decent fuckin guy, and that fuckin Leon got what he deserved... Those poor fuckin dogs. Fuck me, Tommy I woulda skinned that fucker alive if they were mine."

"Yeah...Well, this decent guy is now fucked."

***

Finished with their paperwork and processing at the 5-3 precinct, the detectives loaded Sammy into their car and headed to Central Booking. On the way, they stopped by a coffee shop and Isaacs jumped out to get Sammy a bacon-egg-and-cheese on a Kaiser roll and a light and sweet coffee. Sammy thanked them repeatedly for their kindness.

"Thank you guys again for being so nice. I, I never woulda done that, never--but you seen what he done to my dogs. Man... I loved them dogs. What the fuck was wrong with him? Why'd he have to do this?!" he was almost shouting with grief.

Sammy let the tears flow down his face as he sat in the back of the car, looking out the window at nothing, both detectives feeling his anguish.

"Hey," he said suddenly, "You guys are Irish, right? Either of you gentlemen have one of them little bottles? You know, one of them flasks, with some Irish whiskey I could add to my coffee?" Sammy asked.

Both detectives replied no. Then Isaacs looked over at Tommy and caught his eye. Tommy gave a short nod. "You know, Sammy, maybe we can do you one better," Isaacs offered.

Tommy pulled the car over in front of Shanahan's Pub, an old-timers' bar frequented by Con-Ed men and MTA track-workers, located on 204th Street, just off the Grand Concourse. Shanahan's was a real working man's dive bar that opened at eight in the morning to cater to the neighborhood drunks and third shifters who worked the train yard. They removed Sammy's cuffs and let him out of the car, letting him know in no uncertain terms just how much he would regret even entertaining the thought of escape.

The three men entered the dimly lit pub and walked up to the bar that ran along the left side of the interior. Tommy scanned the room, the tables to the right were empty and the men's room door was open. Sammy climbed onto a bar stool and Keane and Isaacs stood on either side of him. Isaacs ordered three Budweiser's' and three shots of Jameson Irish Whiskey from the grey-haired bartender who walked with a limp and spoke with a brogue.

Keane and Isaacs ordered a few more shots for Sammy, but they each only had one more beer for themselves, intent on sending Sammy off to jail with what would probably be his last drink for a long time.

***

At approximately 10:02 am, two tall, thin men entered the bar with masks on. The leader, wearing a dirty flannel shirt, was brandishing a shotgun and loudly ordered everyone to put their hands on the bar.

It was the third Thursday of the month and these two men knew that there was always extra money in the till to cash the city workers' paychecks. What they didn't expect is that there would be two detectives drinking at the bar on this particular Thursday. What they also didn't know, is that one should keep a safe distance away from the person one is looking to rob or harm, even when holding a shotgun.

The man with the shotgun walked directly up to Isaacs, who still had his hands by his sides, and shouted in his face to put his hands up. Isaacs stared straight through him, as if the masked man wasn't even there, while Keane, in one quick movement, grabbed the barrel of the shotgun and pointed it toward the ceiling, hitting the assailant square in the mouth with his Budweiser. The bottle knocked out his two front teeth and sent him crashing to the floor. Just as quickly, the older Isaacs had a .38 Smith and Wesson held firmly against the skull of the second masked man. Tommy and Isaacs glanced at each other knowingly, and all seemed right with the world.

And all would have been right with the world, except for the fact that Mrs. Alvarez had watched two masked men, armed with what she thought looked like a rifle, enter the bar from her third story window, which was directly across the street from Shanahan's Pub. She called 911 and within minutes several cars showed up to the scene, all from the 5-3, except for one. That one was the unmarked car of Chief Connelly who was on his way to work at One Police Plaza, NYPD headquarters, from his home in Mahopac, NY. He had heard the call come over his radio as he drove south on the Major Deegan Expressway and decided to see how the boys from the 5-3 would handle this job.

***

Four months later, Detective Samuel Isaacs retired from the Police Department, in order to save his pension and avoid a transfer or other punitive action. Sammy Melendez was sent to Riker's Island, where he sat awaiting trial for the murder of Leon Little. Jorge Romans and Miguel Jimenez, the two masked men, pled guilty to the lesser charges of Attempted Robbery 3. Rodriguez was sentenced to two years for being the guy with the gun and Jimenez one year for taking part in the crime. Both were expected to be back on the street in half that time.

Detective Thomas Keane was transferred from his squad in the Bronx to a squad in the 21st Precinct, Manhattan. He was far from happy about his punishment. However, with only a year left until retirement, he knew it could have gone worse. Indeed it could have gone much, much worse than a transfer to a relatively quiet house in Manhattan.

And *worse* had been the intention of Chief Connelly. The chief wanted Detective Thomas Keane sent to Staten

Island, or to "the ass-end of Brooklyn," just to add an extra hour in both directions to Tommy's commute from his White Plains apartment.

But as fate would have it, one of Tommy's dearest friends from the 53rd Precinct was Sergeant Penny Moscowitz, whose mother was the Police Administrative Assistant at One Police Plaza. She was in charge of transfer paperwork. When the transfer order came through, Mrs. Moscowitz recognized Tommy's name and asked her daughter Penny if she should take care of him. Sergeant Moscowitz gave her mother an emphatic yes, and asked her to send him some place safe and easy for him to finish up his career in peace.

Tommy had helped Penny on several occasions when they were both younger and new on the job. During one case in particular, Penny had called for a 10-13 ("Officer Needs Assistance"), while on a foot post on Fordham Road. She had cornered three young men, who had just committed a robbery, but was quickly attacked and overcome by the trio.

They kicked and punched her, and she did everything she could to hold her firearm locked in place in its holster as one of her assailants tried to wrestle it away.

It was Tommy's voice she heard, suddenly mixed in with screams of pain coming from the young men, and the loud thuds and cracks of Tommy's nightstick. From that night on, Penny felt she owed him her life.

Even apart from this incident, Penny had always thought Tommy was a true gentleman, a decent man who was on the job for the right reasons. So if he had bought a murderer a drink, 'Well,' Penny thought to herself, 'He must have deserved that drink.'

So when Penny's mother, PAA Moscowitz, saw the opening for a Squad Detective in the 21st Precinct in Manhattan, she smiled. 'Perfect,' she thought, 'And an easy commute from White Plains. Looks like Chief Connelly's punishment will be a gift to Detective Keane.' She called her daughter right away, quite pleased with herself.

***

Although Tommy would have preferred to finish his career in The Bronx, there was no doubt his new assignment was a gift. Unbeknownst to PAA Moscowitz or the police department, the 2-1 also happened to be Tommy's old neighborhood.

Sister Margaret

Chapter One ~ Fall

Tommy Keane's eyes snapped open to complete darkness. He reached over towards the nightstand and fumbled around for his cellphone to check the time. Eight minutes left before the alarm would sound. He dropped his phone down on the sheet and took a deep and purposeful sigh.

'Fuck, let's get this over with,' he thought to himself. It was time to report to the 21st Precinct to be assigned to a new squad.

The "2-1 Precinct" was located on Manhattan's Upper East Side, home to the ridiculously wealthy, the famous, and the so-called "important" people of the city. It was where you could find Park Avenue, Madison Avenue, 5th Avenue, the "Million Dollar Mile." The 2-1 was a good house, and a relatively quiet one compared to what he was used to in the Bronx, but Tommy was not looking forward to the change. He rubbed his hands over his face and tried not to think about the 5-3 Precinct, where he had started his police career twenty years ago and had been ever since.

Tommy had grown to love that precinct over the last two decades. He felt he was cut out for serving the good people of the Bronx, in their predominantly Puerto Rican and Dominican neighborhoods.

He knew every building, every corner, and every storefront. He recognized every shopkeeper, drug dealer, school principal, parish priest; the good, the bad, and the ugly.

He had an intimate knowledge of the heartbeat of those streets and what made them tick, but all that was over now. Tommy and his partner, Detective Samuel Isaacs, had been caught drinking on duty in a pub near the 5-3 with a man they were responsible for taking to jail for a homicide. No, Detective Keane was not happy about his transfer.

Tommy rolled out of bed and onto the floor and pumped out fifty push-ups, an exercise he did first-thing each and every morning. Afterwards he sat on the edge of his bed and turned on the lamp. His room was the small rear bedroom of his mother's apartment, the same one he and his sister had grown up in. He had kept this room as a crash pad for years, black trash bags taped over the windows to keep out any sign of the sun. As any cop or night shift worker knows, it is impossible to get a proper night's sleep once daylight creeps in.

The bedroom in Tommy's apartment in White Plains was kept the same way, and prior to the divorce, the bedroom windows of his home in Brewster, NY were also blacked out. It was something that his ex-wife, Cookie, couldn't stand. Add that to the late and lonely nights, the hospital visits, and her husband's first marriage (the job itself), and Tommy and Cookie both knew their marriage couldn't last. It was with a great deal of mutual respect that they ended it before it got ugly.

Tommy still loved her, he really loved her a lot, and Cookie adored him, but the job had got in the way. The ghosts of victims past were constantly intruding and they never stopped coming. Being a detective, especially in the Bronx, was like shoveling sand against the tide--one case ended and three more began.

Tommy rubbed at his face again, pushed himself up and stepped out of his room. The haze of cigarette smoke already hung heavily around the living room, snaking its way down the hall to him as he crossed the hallway on the way to the bathroom.

"Good morning, Ma," he called out to his mother before he stepped inside. She was sitting in her recliner, as usual, watching New York 1 News and puffing on a cigarette.

"Morning, Tommy. Remember you have to go to your new precinct today, Tommy. Don't be late, you don't want to make a bad impression on your first day Tommy. Tommy? Can I make you something to eat before you leave? Something for breakfast maybe or maybe some lunch Tommy? Can I do that for you, Tommy?"

"No Ma, I'm fine. But thanks."

"Okay Tommy, but I asked. Remember that I asked when you get hungry later, Tommy."

"I will Ma and I love you for asking."

Mrs. Keane was in the very early stages of Dementia, or at least that is what the doctor had said. Tommy wasn't so sure he was right as it seemed like her memory was actually as sharp as it had ever been. But to him, and his sister Kathleen, there was a certain something increasingly off about their mother's mental state. She was very much still herself. She still enjoyed a Scotch, or twelve, every day, and went through a pack of Marlboro a day as well, but there was something changing. She was more compulsive about things, one of which was addressing everyone she spoke to by name, several times, in every sentence.

He made a mental note to call his sister to discuss their mother and see about getting her another appointment with the doctor.

***

Tommy stepped out of the building and stood on the stoop, looking left and then right, scanning the street before taking a deep breath of the crisp October air. 'It's a fine morning,' he thought. Even if he didn't care to face the day, it was still a fine morning.

Tommy walked the twenty plus blocks to the 21st Precinct from his mother's building on 88th Street, taking Second Avenue most of the way down. He had walked these blocks thousands of times in his life and he had a hundred stories he could tell about every corner, every storefront and stoop along the way. Funny though, in a way, he now felt like a stranger on these streets. He had lived in the neighborhood for more than seventeen years, but with the speed at which things change in Manhattan, it felt as though it could have been sixty.

So many places were gone. Most of the old German restaurants were gone: The Ideal on 86th Street where he ate at least once a week as a young man had been gone for at least fifteen, maybe twenty years now, he thought. Many of the old Irish Pubs like Flemings and Fitzpatrick's had long closed their doors, and the once numerous Hungarian restaurants and Italian delis were all gone, too.

The Boys Club on the corner--the old-time soda shop where an old man with a cigar hanging out of his mouth pumped syrup into a glass and filled it with soda water--that was gone, too. The Kings Menswear, and Thom McCann shoe store that he remembered were both gone, along with the friendly neighborhood "hello." He remembered when he couldn't walk a block in Yorkville without saying hello to ten different people; today no one would even look you in the eye. Yes, the old neighborhood had certainly changed.

There was a time when the Upper East Side was known by its neighborhoods: Yorkville, Lenox Hill, Carnegie Hill, but that familiarity was all gone too, like the German Restaurants and the smiles. The rents were too high for the restaurants to stay and too high for the working class masses who had once filled the old tenements that lined the streets, from Lexington Avenue to York.

The old man bars were now empty during the day, most of their clientele deceased, and now these establishments catered to the younger, hipper crowd willing to pay $7.50 for a domestic beer and twice that for a call drink.

'What the fuck,' Tommy thought, 'Is forty-six that old? Am I really that much of a fucking dinosaur?'

He arrived at the 2-1 Precinct early, ID'd himself at the desk, and made his way up to the squad room on the second floor. Tommy had been in the precinct before and knew his way around but was pleasantly surprised to see that it had been renovated. No one took notice of him as he walked to the stairwell and went upstairs. There wasn't anyone at the PAA desk so he went inside to the office of the Squad Room Commander, Lieutenant Kevin Bricks. The door was open so he knocked on the wooden door jamb.

"Lu? Tommy Keane, I'm your new man."

"Tom, come on in and grab a seat!" Lieutenant Bricks exclaimed as if they were old friends. "Good to meet you, Tom. I've heard nothing but good things. I know why you are here, and I know you're not too happy about it, but relax. It's a fairly quiet house, crime-wise not complaint-wise… believe me, you'll have plenty of cases to keep you busy, but nothing too heavy, not like you're used to in the Bronx. It will be an easy place for you to end your career." He leaned back in his chair, "John Haynes put in a good word for you also. He didn't have to though, your reputation precedes you."

"John's a good man," Tommy replied.

"Fuck yeah he is," said Bricks. "I've heard you're a good worker, Tom, an active cop, and a stand-up guy. You'll be joining B-Squad and start catching cases tomorrow. Oh and you'll have to share a desk, we have no room in this dump."

"Yeah, was the same in the 5-3."

"Unfortunately you'll have to meet the Precinct Commander today--he's a tight ass prick. A Queens Marine prodigy," Lieutenant Bricks smirked, "He hit every test just right and made Captain with all of twenty-seven collars, twenty-six of which were misdemeanors." He shook his head slowly. "I'm sure he's gonna break your shoes about your trouble up in the 5-3. Just do the ol' 'yes sir no sir' and you'll be back in the swing of things tomorrow, cool?"

"Absolutely," Tommy replied.

He stood up and shook hands with Lieutenant Bricks.

"Thanks Lu, I really appreciate it."

"Doreen!" Lieutenant Bricks shouted out his office door. Doreen Doyle stepped into the doorway.

"Yeah Lu?"

"This is Tom Keane. He's now on B-Squad with you. See if you have some desk room for him and stick him on rotation. He starts catching tomorrow."

"You got it, Lu," Doreen replied. She stuck her hand out and shook Tommy's firmly, "Doreen Doyle, nice ta meet ya."

Then she turned and headed back into the main squad room with Tommy following.

"There is zero desk space here, but you can share with me until something opens up. I'm flying solo today cause the other guys have court, but I'm going to head out to do a couple interviews if you want to come along?"

"Sure, but I have to meet with the captain first."

"Okay, I'll meet you outside in the grey Crown Vic. It's parked right out front."

***

Captain Joseph Peleggi was everything Lieutenant Kevin Bricks said he was and more. A twenty-two year company man from Port Washington, Long Island, he had been a cop in Queens with an empty-suit reputation. He took and passed his first Sergeants exam, and soon after, took and passed the Lieutenant's exam, and then again the Captain's exam, the rank in which he would spend the rest of his career.

All positions above Captain were made by appointment and not granted through civil service exams. And if there was a certainty in Joseph Peleggi's police career, it was that he had no friends in the Police Department, so the chance of a political appointment to a higher rank was slim to none.

He was simply one of those people who were impossible to like. If there was one thing that he was good at though, it was micro management. Joseph Peleggi knew the ins and outs of everything that happened in his precinct. He was a COMPSTAT prince. Whenever called upon by a supervisor at COMPSTAT--the command statistics meetings down at One Police Plaza where the Chiefs and Commissioner would grill precinct commanders on their crime stats--Peleggi always shined. He always had an answer ready, and if it wasn't the right answer, well then he always had a scapegoat he could throw to the lions as an answer to why statistics, investigations, or activities were not going as they should. He was a miserable cunt and everyone knew it... even he did.

Tommy came down the battered stairs and stepped into the lobby. The noises were the same here as in the 5-3: phones ringing, keyboard keys tapping, victims crying, and crooks arguing. He briefly made eye contact with a woman sitting on the stone bench, her purse held tightly in her lap. Her nose wrinkled against the putrid smell coming off the drunk sitting next to her.

Tommy felt a pang of sympathy for her as he walked to the captain's door. He showed the detective shield he wore on his belt, and nodded at the desk sergeant as he reached for the knob.

The sergeant widened his eyes and shook his head fiercely while raising a hand to Tommy. He gestured for Tommy to come to the desk with a jerk of his head. Tommy approached the desk and the sergeant lowered his head and spoke in a low voice.

"I have to announce you." He rolled his eyes slightly and then repeated it, "I have to announce you. It's a thing. Who may I say is calling, Detective?" He said with the slightest hint of embarrassment and sarcasm. Tommy paused.

"Detective Tommy Keane," he replied.

"Tommy Keane, I've heard of you. Nice to meet you. Dominic Ruffalo. I was a cop in the 4-9 before I got promoted."

They shook hands over the tall sergeant's desk, and Sergeant Ruffalo picked up the phone.

"Yes sir, Sergeant Ruffalo speaking. I have a Detective Tommy Keane here to see you, sir." He listened a moment and then put the phone down. "Go ahead in," Sergeant Ruffalo said shaking his head slightly as he looked back down at his log book.

Tommy knocked twice on the door and then entered Captain Peleggi's office.

"Good morning, Captain. Detective Tommy Keane, sir."

The office was stuffy and warm as if the air never circulated. The small room contained too many articles of furniture for the space and was dominated by a large desk, in front of which sat two grey metal arm chairs with dark green padding.

"Yes, Detective Keane, I've been expecting you. Take a seat, Detective. I'm a very busy man so let's get straight to the point and abandon all pleasantries. I know all about what happened in the 5-3 and why you are here. I know you don't want to be here, and I want you to know I don't care to have you here in the 2-1 either. I don't have room or patience for cowboys, or short-timers, who don't care about their jobs or procedures. You may have had an exemplary arrest record in the Bronx, and I know you are highly decorated, and I know about your shootings. I even know you caught the Push Button Rapist and what happened to your partner in that Narcotics shooting."

He raised a hand to wipe spittle from the corner of his mouth as he continued on with his speech.

"You are a veteran, a paratrooper no less, and you obviously have many friends, or fans, in this department, but none of that means shit to me. I want to make it crystal clear that if I were in command of the 5-3 at the time of the

Melendez incident, I would have seen that you were fired. I want you to understand that we have no room in today's police department for anything outside of standard operating procedure. Now, you may fancy yourself some kind of tough guy, maybe even a hero of some sort, but let me tell you, Detective, if you so much as step out of line once, or think you are going to lay down for the next thirteen months--yes, I know how much time you have left--I will do everything in my power to see that you leave this job without your pension. Do I make myself clear, Detective?"

"Yes sir, crystal clear," Tommy replied.

"Do you have anything to say, Detective?"

Tommy, with his monotone voice and deadpan stare, replied, "I'll do a good job for you, Captain."

Captain Peleggi, somewhat disappointed he wasn't able to get a rise out of Tommy, looked down at his paperwork.

"You may leave now, Detective."

Tommy hesitated a moment until the Captain looked up. Their eyes met.

"Thank you sir, it was nice meeting you this morning." He held his gaze for a moment longer, then stood and walked out of the office.

Chapter Two

Tommy stepped out of the precinct onto the stoop and looked left, then right, scanning the block. He saw Detective Doreen Doyle a few car lengths up, leaning against a battered silver Crown Vic. He went down the precinct steps, making his way towards the car, skirting around a double-parked moving van.

Doreen Doyle was thirty-two years old and approximately five foot eight. She wore a navy pantsuit that made her look like a politician, a grade school principal, or maybe exactly what she was, a detective for the New York City Police Department. Doreen Doyle was not beautiful. She was an average plain-looking woman, but she had a nice shade of strawberry blonde hair, bright green eyes, and freckles scattered across her nose and cheeks that not only screamed 'Irish Girl from Queens' but also made her look younger than she was. She also had an infectious smile that would enliven any conversation. She didn't look as hard as one would expect a NYPD Detective to look, or nearly as hard as she was.

Doreen joined the cops at the age of twenty-one. She came from a working class family in Sunnyside Queens and got three years of college under her belt before dropping out and joining the Police Academy. For seven years, she worked in the Housing Bureau in Brooklyn, where she patrolled the projects in Police Service Area 2. Her record was solid but not exemplary; she was never in trouble, and she always did what she was supposed to do.

One day, on a hot and humid August afternoon, she and her partner went out on a call for a family dispute in the Brownsville houses. When they arrived at the apartment they could hear screaming and children crying, and the neighbors were gathered in the hallway.

"He gonna kill her! He gonna kill her fo sho this time!" The elderly woman closest to the door yelled at the cops as soon as she saw them.

Both Doyle and her partner, Victor Hernandez, rushed into the apartment where one Tre Moore was holding his live-in girlfriend, Teesha Jones, the mother of two of his four children, to the floor and punching her already battered and bloodied face.

Officers Hernandez and Doyle simultaneously pulled Tre Moore from the badly beaten Teesha Jones, wrestled him to the floor, and cuffed him. While both officers sat on their knees catching their breath, Teesha Jones appeared from the kitchen covered in her own blood and hurled a frying pan full of hot oil onto Officer Doreen Doyle. She then slammed the heavy cast iron pan into the head of Officer Hernandez knocking him unconscious.

Doreen Doyle, in extreme pain, leapt onto Teesha Jones' back and, in almost a single motion, drove Teesha's head into the cinderblock wall behind her, rendering her unconscious. As she was cuffing Miss Jones, she realized Tre Moore had taken advantage of the scuffle and had made a run for it, pushing past the neighbors who had been standing on the threshold watching the brawl.

Officer Doyle immediately gave pursuit into the hallway, radioing a 10-13 (Officer Needs Assistance) into Central; as Tre Moore attempted to wrestle open the door to the staircase with his cuffed hands behind his back. Officer Doyle struck him across the head with her firearm, knocking him to his knees, and then struck him again for good measure, while forcing him to lay down face first in the hallway. She kept her weapon pointed at him while she returned to the entrance of the apartment and called out to Victor Hernandez. He answered after the second call.

Both officers, and the two prisoners, were removed from the scene and taken to Brookdale Hospital to be treated. Officer Hernandez received seven stitches to the back of the head, Tre Moore received twelve stitches to his head from the blows he received from Officer Doyle, and Teesha Jones was held for observation before she and Tre Moore were taken to Central Booking and, ultimately, Rikers Island.

Officer Doreen Doyle was treated for second- and third-degree burns. These burns would leave the back of her neck, the back of her right shoulder and her right arm permanently disfigured.

Officer Hernandez received a Medal of Merit. Officer Doyle was awarded the Medal of Commendation and permitted to choose where she would be assigned next. She asked to be moved to a detective squad, and was subsequently transferred to the 2-1.

For her heroism in saving her partner and the four children while simultaneously apprehending two dangerous criminals, Officer Doyle was promoted to Detective Third Grade.

***

Doreen was leaning against the car looking at her phone when Tommy reached her. She looked up and pushed off the car.

"You wanna drive, Tom?"

"No, you can drive, Doyle," Tommy replied, opening the passenger side door while Doreen went around to the driver's side.

"I've got a couple of interviews to do: a robbery at the Junior High School on 76th and then a fraud on 80th. After, you wanna drive around and get a feel for the neighborhood?"

"No, not necessary. I think after your 80th Street interview, we head over to Italian Village on First Avenue. I'll buy you lunch and you can give me the skinny on the squad and the precinct? How's that sound? Cool?"

"Italian Village? So you're already familiar with the neighborhood then?" Doreen replied.

"A little," Tommy said in his low monotone voice, staring straight out the window.

"Okay. But before I give you … the skinny… on the squad, how bout you give me the skinny on you? I understand you have a big rep in the Bronx, a man's man, a bit of a hero they say."

"Don't believe everything you hear. In fact, don't believe anything you hear," he replied.

"I don't. I never believe anything I hear and only half of what I see," Doreen said with a cocky smirk.

"Well then, you have the makings of a good detective."

"The makings of?" She turned toward him with a frown, "What makes you think I'm not a good detective already?"

"I'm sure you are a fine detective, Doyle," Tommy replied. "As far as the skinny on me, what are they saying and what do you want to know? I'm easy, you can ask me anything. I won't be insulted, and if I don't like the question I won't answer it."

Doreen pulled the Crown Vic into an open spot by a fire hydrant in front of the two red doors of the Junior High school. She put the car in park and turned towards Tommy with a grin.

"Okay fun!" Doreen replied, "I heard about why they sent you here, is it true?"

"Well, it's true that I took a decent guy out for a drink before I sent him to jail. Yes that's true and I am guilty... But I feel no guilt."

"Okay, I also heard you've killed more men than cancer up there in the Bronx, that true?"

"Nope, that's bullshit. Most all that Wild West stuff is bullshit. Listen, the Bronx is a busy place and if you're an active cop you're eventually gonna step in some shit. My old partner and I were active cops and active detectives when we went to Narcotics. Plenty of guys worked every bit as hard as we did, even harder, so no there's no hero in this car, except for maybe you, Doyle." Tommy grinned at her, "But there's definitely no hero in this seat."

"I remember hearing about when your partner got his eye shot out. You took one in the shoulder, then chased the perps to the roof and got into a gunfight with them. That's gotta be true cause I read about that in the papers."

"That's mostly true, Doyle. Just mostly true."

Doyle threw the police parking placard on the dash and they both climbed out of the car, heading toward the entrance to the Junior High.

"Interesting," replied Doyle, "Now it gets interesting. You married?"

"Divorced."

"Kids?"

"One. A daughter. She's going to be nineteen."

"Wow nineteen. Seems a little old for you. How old are you, Tom?"

"Old enough to have a nineteen year old daughter, Doyle."

This question and answer session went on for a couple of hours, during and after Doreen Doyle's interviews, and into their meal time. Following the interview with a possible eye-witness in Doreen's fraud case on 80th and Madison Avenue, they climbed back into the Crown Vic.

Doreen then drove them over to First Avenue and parked the car in the bus stop between 79th and 80th Streets. Upon entering Italian Village, she saw the owner in his red and white pizza man shirt come out from behind the counter with a big smile on. This made her feel welcome and she was happy to be remembered.

"Tommy! Tommy itsa so good to see you, Tommy. Where hava you beena?" Tony, the owner, exclaimed as he passed by Doreen and hugged Tommy, shaking his hand vigorously.

Doreen's eyes opened wide and her jaw dropped. She cocked her head and stared at Tommy as she sat down at a table near the counter and listened to Tommy and Tony exchange pleasantries.

"Okaya ok, let me get backa ta work," Tony said in his heavy Italian accent, heading back around the glass-fronted counter.

"Doreen," Tommy said, "C'mon, let's sit in the back there."

"They only open the back room for dinner," replied Doreen.

"Hey Tony, it's okay we sit in the back?" Tommy asked.

"Tommy, you sita any place a you like."

"Thanks, Tony," Tommy replied, smiling.

Doreen gave Tommy a disbelieving look as they took seats at a clothed table for four in the back room. They had the dim room to themselves and barely heard the clatter from the front pizzeria area.

"So what's the story here, Tom?" Doreen asked.

"Nope. It's your turn, Doyle. Give me the low down on this command. I already have a read on the Captain and the Lu seems like a decent guy. What can you tell me about the rest of the squad?"

"The Lu is a real decent guy, a really good man," Doreen replied sitting back in her seat. "Sergeant Browne? He's the Squad Sergeant and is a bit of a dick. He sucks up to the Lu and the Captain all the time. He's gonna suck up to you also when he meets you." She nodded, "He's just that way, ya know, he's weak. I don't trust him and not cause I think he's a rat or looking to score points. It's just that, well, he's weak and always says the wrong thing, or maybe says too much, and usually about something he knows nothing about."

A waitress came out of the back kitchen door, and--slightly surprised to see people sitting in the closed dining room--took their orders and retreated to get their food and drinks.

Doreen continued, "Our team is good. You got lucky, I think. Mark Stein is a smart detective, he's about your age, maybe a little older, and about your time on I think. Jimmy Colletti is also a good guy, he's the youngest in the squad. His father was a Chief and his brother is a Captain in the 2-8. His heart is in the right place, and he likes to work... He's just a little green."

"And you?" Tommy asked, "What can you tell me about you?"

"Well, I'm the best detective in the precinct," she said with a smirk. "Actually no, Stein is the best detective in the precinct. He's taught me a lot and he's got a good heart. I like Stein and I think you will too."

"Married?"

"Stein? Yes."

"No, you," Tommy replied, with a half-smile.

"Me no. Almost once but that didn't work out so well."

"Sorry."

"Don't be, he was a mama's boy, kinda a spoiled brat. It never would have worked in the end. I'm glad it fell apart."

Doyle finished up her slice with mushrooms and Tommy his chicken parmesan on garlic bread. When they received a radio call of a robbery outside the Barnes and Noble on 86th Street, both stood up and started toward the front door. Tommy left a $20 bill on the table for the waitress. Doreen, noticing it, thought, 'Wow, that's an excessive tip.'

"What do I owe you, Tony?" Tommy asked the owner on the way out.

"Nothin for you, Tommy, nothin for you."

"Thank you, Tony. It was good to see you today."

"Tommy, come again soona my friend, pleasea we missa you."

When they reached the parked car, Doyle asked, "So, you always buy people lunch places where you don't have to pay?"

"He's a good guy, Tony is, and we go back a ways."

"I can see that," responded Doyle as she started up the car.

The call turned out to be a fight between two high school students. The "robbery" part was one kid throwing the other's backpack into the middle of the street. The detectives left the kids with the patrol officers, who were already on the scene, and headed back to the Station House.

Sister Margaret

Chapter Three

After his tour finished later that afternoon, Tommy started his walk back to his mother's apartment, heading east to First Avenue and then turning north toward 88th Street. When he reached 73rd Street, he stopped in for a bite at Finnegan's Wake Pub, a place he had known for over thirty years. It was a neighborhood staple, and had been a favorite haunt of his mother's back when she left the house regularly and still cared to be out and about. These days she rarely wanted to leave the front stoop, much less the block, other than to do the shopping or go to the doctor.

Tommy found a spot at the bar, just inside the front door, and ordered himself a Budweiser and a shepherd's pie from the short, round bartender. Finnegan's Wake, a bit of a throwback of a traditional New York City Irish pub, had probably seen its heyday in the 1980's but still managed to bring in an older crowd of local neighborhood people, who enjoyed the cheap food and reasonable drink prices.

The pub had an overall tired atmosphere, from the low ceilings and the dank lighting, to the dusty shelves and the weary faces, but Tommy liked stopping into these old places because they were just that, old.

There was a familiar feel, a smell, and a comfort that old neighborhood places had, something that simply couldn't be replicated, no matter how hard new places tried. 'Nothing compares to an old Pub that is weathered and worn and has stood the test of time,' Tommy thought.

As he looked around the bar and into the small dining area to his left, he recognized a face or two but didn't know anyone by name. He found his shepherd's pie to be dry, and somewhat stale, much like the ambiance in the room. He pushed his plate away and finished his second beer, leaving a tip for the bartender and walking out with a wave.

Back outside he scanned the Avenue briefly, right then left, before continuing north, not really thinking about his first day at his new precinct, or of Doyle, Lieutenant Bricks, his new captain, or the remaining thirteen months he had left until retirement.

Tommy had that ability--when he had nothing pressing or important to think about, he could almost go into a state of meditation. He was well aware of his surroundings but mentally he would be completely without thought, without worry, or desire of any sort.

Conversely, when he had a job, a mission, a task to do, it was almost all-enveloping and his mind would wrap itself around the problem or mystery until the situation was satisfied. Tommy was a true problem solver, a pragmatist at an elite level.

He walked along First Avenue and he came up on another old haunt, American Trash. Another place that had been open for decades, this joint was just that, a joint. It had started out as an intentional dive bar in the 1980's and simply maintained the vibe for the last thirty years.

Tommy slowed his step and skirted around a couple heading south. He opened the door and went in, looking at the eight customers in the place and recognizing no one. The bar looked exactly the same as he remembered: the same neon signs, and the same myriad of crap hanging on the walls. He went up to the bar and caught the eye of the young, tattooed, barmaid with multi-colored hair. She headed over to him and he asked her if Ian still worked there.

"Yeah. Are you a friend of Ian's? He works tomorrow night," she smiled a pretty smile with her pierced lips, "Can I get you something?"

Tommy replied "No, thank you, I was just checking to see if Ian was in."

"Are you sure I can't get you something? I'm sure you'll find me a little more interesting than Ian," she shot back with a sweet smile and a somewhat seductive look in her eye.

"I'm sorry, not tonight, love. Though I'm sure I would," Tommy replied with a wink.

"Okay, well, you know where to come if you get thirsty," she said as Tommy headed back toward the door and she watched him leave.

Tommy stepped back out onto the street. He scanned the block right and left before proceeding north again. Once he made it to 85th Street, he took a left onto the side street and walked up to Ryan's Daughter Pub, yet another old haunt. Tommy and his friends would drink in this place when they were underage. It, like most of the pubs left in the neighborhood, had gone through some changes. They no longer served food and now in the evenings they catered to a much younger and more obnoxious crowd than Tommy cared to be around.

But this walk he was taking was a bit nostalgic. Tommy didn't consciously realize it but he was searching for some sense of grounding, an old friend in an old haunt to make him feel that he somehow, once again, belonged to this neighborhood.

Ryan's Daughter was also quiet this evening and the only face he recognized belonged to loudmouth Jimmy Leary, a balding grey-haired man in his mid-sixties. Leary was a retired city bus driver who would talk nonstop nonsense to anyone who had the patience to listen. He was known in the neighborhood as Leary Da Mouth, or just Da Mouth to most. Tommy wasn't about to give him his ear so he quickly did an about-face and headed for the door, when he heard Da Mouth shout behind him.

"Tommy Keane! Oh! Tommy Keane is that you?"

Tommy just kept walking, pretending he didn't hear.

One block east, on the corner of 85th and York, was Bailey's Corner Pub. Tommy always liked stopping in there as a few of his old friends frequented the place, and it was only three blocks down from his mother's. Both Tommy and his mother still referred to it as Nash's, as its previous name was Nash's Cash Box.

As Tommy approached the entrance to the bar, he looked across the street to Arturo's Restaurant and mumbled to himself, "Fuck, I shoulda ate there," the flavor of dry shepherd's pie repeating on him. Arturo's was another old Neighborhood institution, where Tommy had had many, many meals over the years and the occasional family-function in their downstairs room. 'Ah shit,' he thought, 'A little Chicken Rollatini would have hit the spot tonight… next time.'

He entered Bailey's Corner and scanned the room, allowing his eyes to adjust to the dimness. He recognized a face or two but no old friends or acquaintances here. The only person he knew by name was Jack, the bartender. Jack made eye contact and gave the slight head nod and brow raise that said, "Hello, how are you and welcome," without a word.

Tommy grabbed a stool at the near end of the bar, took his black leather car coat off and hung it over the back of it. He smiled to himself as he sat under the sign reading, *Failte romat isteac*, ("Welcome" in Gaelic), finally feeling a sense of comfort and belonging this evening.

'Yes,' he thought, 'There is joy, delight, and welcome before me,' just as Jack placed an ice cold bottle of Budweiser and a shot of Jameson in front of him.

"Tommy, good to see you. How ya been?" Jack leaned forward, resting his elbow on the bar.

"Never better, Jacky boy, never better. How are you doing today my friend?"

"Things are good, Tommy. You down visiting your Ma today? How's she makin out?"

"Yeah, you could say that… She's doing great, thanks."

"Tell her I said hi, Tommy," Jack said as he went to serve another customer.

Jack was a fan of Tommy's. Tommy was a good solid tipper--which any bartender will tell you is the true measure of a man--but he was also a good drinker. It wasn't that he would often drink to excess but that he was always even tempered, polite, and fairly quiet. He always had a kind word or a sarcastic quip, and was easily able to engage in intelligent conversation. He was definitely the sort of customer Jack enjoyed having in the place.

Tommy sipped his beer and looked around the bar, allowing memories to overtake him. He remembered being here with his sister, Kathleen, and a large group of friends at an after-wedding party. He could almost hear their teasing and laughter. Jack returned to his end of the bar and Tommy returned to the present.

Tommy sat for a couple of hours and enjoyed a few more beers and another shot, watched Jack schmooze with his customers, and occasionally joined in on the banter with Jack and some of the other patrons. Then, he decided to call it a night and said a warm good-bye to Jack, promising to stop in again soon.

He returned to his mother's apartment on 88th Street and let himself in, trying to turn the four locks on the door as quietly as possible so as to not wake his mother with their tumbling. He was always careful, but she was rarely sleeping when he arrived home. She started talking to him as soon as he closed the front door.

"Tommy? Tommy, how was your first day at the 2-1 Tommy? Did you make any new friends? Tommy did you arrest anyone today Tommy? Is that why you are so late, Tommy?"

"No Ma, I didn't arrest anyone today. All the new kids at school were nice to me. I stopped by Nash's on the way home and had a beer with Jack, that's why I'm a little late."

He took off his coat and hung it over the back of the chair then perched on the arm of the couch next to his mother's recliner. As usual, she was sitting comfortably in a faded blue flannel nightgown. The glow from the television illuminated the smoke from her cigarette, which was resting in the ashtray.

"Ohhh, how is that Jack, Tommy? He's such a fine young man, isn't he Tommy?"

"Yeah Ma, he is a good fella. What are you up to tonight?"

"I've just been watching some television tonight, Tommy. I watched some 'All in the Family' and some 'Andy Griffith,' Tommy, I got tired of the news and all those awful terrorists. Your police department should do more to fight terrorists Tommy. Those dirty bastards are everywhere Tommy, they took over France and they're naming all the little English boys in England Mohammed now Tommy. I think you need to meet with your commissioner or your captain about that Tommy. It isn't right."

"Okay Ma, first thing in the morning I'll look into that for you, okay? Can I get you something from the kitchen before I go to bed, Ma?"

"No Tommy, I'm gonna watch another program and go to bed myself."

"Okay Ma, I love you."

"I love you Tommy, sleep good Tommy. You'll need a good night's sleep for your big day tomorrow Tommy."

Tommy went into his bedroom. 'My big day?' he thought to himself. She was a sweet crazy old girl but he also worried that he'd have to get with her doctor soon to see where this was heading.

Sister Margaret

Chapter Four

Tommy's eyes snapped open to the complete darkness of his bedroom. He reached for his phone on the nightstand and checked the time. He had ten minutes until the alarm went off. He sighed and stretched in bed, then rolled over, dropped onto the floor and did his fifty push-ups.

He headed into the bathroom to shower and shave and then got dressed in the typical fashion of most detectives-- simple sport coat, shirt and tie, and leather lace-up Oxfords.

Tommy always took pride in his appearance, as he did in the Army, and while he was in uniform patrol for the NYPD. He never purchased expensive designer clothing but did always have everything tailored so it fit properly.

With a slight taper to his trousers and a well fitted sport coat he always looked sharp and put together with more of an athletic look than one would expect from an off-the-rack JC Penney ensemble.

He headed into the living room to grab his coat and said good-bye to his mother on the way, kissing her on top of her grey-haired head, as she watched 'New York 1 News.'

Not taking her eyes off of the television, she called, "Have a good day, Tommy. Be careful Tommy and remember the terrorists Tommy. I don't want you to forget to ask the Commissioner about the terrorists, okay Tommy?" letting out a breath of smoke from her cigarette as she spoke.

"Ok Ma, I won't. I'll be sure to give the commissioner your advice... Have a good day love, and don't wait up for me again, okay?"

Tommy took the pre-war marble stairs down to the first floor and stepped out onto the stoop, looking left and then right, scanning the block. He decided to walk down Second Avenue so he could stop into H&H Bagels on 80th Street and pick up a small spread for the office. A sort of "Hello" to B Squad, a "Glad to be with you."

He entered the narrow shop and was engulfed in the warmth and smell of fresh-baked bagels. The line snaked from the back counter all the way to the front door, and Tommy gladly took his spot in the back to await his turn.

***

In typical Keane fashion he was the first to arrive in the office, so he put out the bagels, butter, and cream cheese and sat down at Doyle's desk to wait for the rest of the squad to filter in. The first was Jimmy Colletti, a well-dressed, young, twenty-eight-year-old. He had broad shoulders and a broad smile.

"Tom Keane?" he asked.

"Tommy," Keane replied.

"Hey, nice to meet you, Tommy." Colletti leaned over the worn metal desk to shake Tommy's hand. "I heard you'd be joining us. Sorry I missed you yesterday, I had court. Hey, you bring in these bagels?"

Tommy nodded.

"Great thanks. I ran out of the house so early, I didn't have time to grab anything."

Just as Jimmy was finishing his sentence and grabbing one of the plain bagels, Detective Mark Stein entered the squad room. He didn't say anything to anyone, just hung his worn and tired trench coat on the coat rack and slowly proceeded toward his desk, which was directly opposite Doyle's.

He made a deep sigh and sat down across from Tommy, still not making eye contact. He pushed his ugly glasses up on his nose as he reached into his desk for a file and said, still not looking up at Tommy, "Detective Keane, I presume? Welcome to the 2-1. This ain't the Bronx, as I'm sure you know. I hope you don't find it boring. If I can tell you anything about this place, it's don't lose your patience with the wealthy who live around here, and don't lose your patience with the brass either, cause their both gonna test you... your patience that is."

"Thanks for the advice... Detective Stein, I presume?"

Stein looked up and over the top of his glasses at Tommy and gave him a sly smile.

Stein had heard about Tommy, both from the papers and from other cops, and he understood him to be a stand-up guy and a good worker, something he thought their squad could use.

He very much liked Doyle and Colletti, but both were still fairly green as far as their investigative skills were concerned, and both were also much younger that Stein. At forty-nine, most of his contemporaries had already retired, so inside he quietly welcomed this newcomer. He hoped for a new colleague who could be his equal; he was tired of being the elder statesman of the squad.

Mark Stein was the father of two girls, who were both out of college, and he and his wife had been married for twenty-six years. Stein had started his police career when he was twenty-one, right after graduating from SUNY Oneonta.

His first assignment was in Harlem, where, after nine years, he was promoted to Detective and then transferred to the Manhattan Sex Crimes Unit (now Special Victims), where he worked for almost ten years before putting in for a transfer. From there, he landed in the 2-1, where he had been for the last eight years. Stein was a Second Grade Detective who had twenty-seven years on the job and who hoped to make First Grade before his retirement.

He moved slowly, and he spoke slowly, but his intellect was fast and sharp--he was an excellent and highly respected detective despite the fact that he looked and dressed like an out-of-work insurance salesman.

Lieutenant Bricks and Doyle walked into the squad room together.

"Good morning men," the Lu announced upon entrance. "I see everyone has met our new man, Tommy Keane. Tommy's coming to us from the 5-3 in the Bronx. He's got lots of experience and he's gonna be a fine addition. Please show him everything he needs to know about the 21st and--Oh! Where'd these bagels come from?"

"Tommy brought them in, Lu," Colletti stated with his mouth full.

"Tommy! Look at you making friends already. Alright, go to work everyone. Is Browne in yet?" Lieutenant Bricks asked the room in general.

"Not yet, Lu," Colletti replied.

"Okay, tell him I need to see him when he shows."

The Lieutenant walked into his office with a bagel and closed the door behind him.

"Oooh bagels, fun! Thanks Tommy," said Doyle as Tommy got up to give her the seat to her desk. "No it's okay, go ahead and sit. I don't need to sit just yet."

Just then, Charice Tate, the squad's PAA, walked in with the morning's assignments--cases from the night before to distribute to each of the detectives. She eyed Keane and headed straight towards him.

"New D.T.? You catching today, handsome man?" she drawled, with a bit of sass as she half-sat on the edge of the desk swinging her black braids away from her face.

"Yes ma'am I am," Tommy replied with a smile.

"Well good, there ain't nothing to it but to jump right in with both feet, honey. I'm Charice, if you need anything you just ask me honey, okay? This one's too old to know what's goin on and he don't care anyhows." She pointed toward Stein. "These two are babes still. Sergeant Browne, well don't even get me started on his sorry ass. And my man, Lieutenant Bricks, he don't need no questions, that man needs a nap and a vacation. So you just come to Charice first if you have questions, Detective, and I'll take care of ya."

"Well thank you, Charice. It's so very nice to meet you."

"The pleasure is all mine, Detective, and I'm glad you're a good looking Detective too. We need more of those, don't we, Detective Doyle?"

"It don't hurt, Charice," Doyle added.

"Hey, what's wrong with this specimen? I know Stein is a dinosaur, but don't tell me you ladies are hurting for eye candy when I walk into the room," Colletti teased. Doyle snickered as Charice went on.

"Colletti, you is way too young for Charice. This building needs more *men*. Proper grown men. You cute and all, but a woman likes a man with some years, some experience." And on that note, she sashayed out of the room, back to her desk by the squad's entrance.

"Every morning," Doyle said to Keane, rolling her eyes with a sigh.

As soon as PAA Charice left the room, Sergeant Browne walked in.

"Good morning, all," He announced to the room in general as he walked over to Doyle's desk where Tommy still sat.

"Detective Keane? I'm Sergeant Browne, Squad Sergeant here. Nice to meet you."

Tommy stood and the two men shook hands.

"Nice to meet you, Sergeant Browne."

"Hey, give me a minute and then join me in my office?" He nodded towards a closed door tucked in the corner of the squad room. "We'll go over how we do things here at the 2-1."

"Absolutely," Tommy replied.

The Sergeant walked into his office and closed the door behind him, and Tommy sat back down at Doyle's desk. He opened his first official 21st Precinct case file: An "assault three," with a known perp from a dispute in a frozen yogurt stand.

An employee had thrown a cup of frozen yogurt at a customer, causing a minor eye injury, before quitting and leaving the store. Tommy shook his head to himself, bit into a bagel, and sighed. 'Easy one, it's an easy one. This shoulda been squashed by patrol and shoulda never made it to the squad. But hey, can't complain about the easy ones,' he thought.

Just then Lieutenant Bricks' door flew open and he stepped into the squad room.

"Okay everyone, listen up. We got a homicide up on 93rd Street. All of you get your shit together and head up there right now. Stein, this is your case but Keane is with you on it. It's a serious one and the press is gonna be all over it, so get your asses up there and make sure patrol has everything blocked off. And no one gets in or out. A nun has been murdered at Our Lady of Perpetual Hope and it's supposed to be pretty bad. Doyle, you come with me. Stein, Keane, and Colletti, you men meet us up there. Let's go. Let's hustle it up. Browne! Sergeant Browne!" Lieutenant Bricks yelled, "We got a homicide, it's gonna be a press case. Try and keep a hold on things here, keep everything under wraps... we don't know anything yet. And stay in constant contact, you got that?"

"You got it, Lu," Sergeant Browne replied from his doorway.

'A press case,' Tommy thought, 'three words detectives hate the most.'

A press case is just that, something that the press will want to write about, something with juice. Not every homicide case was considered newsworthy, in Tommy's experience. There had been weeks in the Bronx with a murder or two every day and not a single mention in any of the papers.

'Shit,' Tommy went on in his head. 'The only time anything makes the news in the Bronx is when a cop does something wrong. And even then most of that shit doesn't make the paper either. So much for sitting on my hands for the next thirteen months.'

The three men raced up to the scene. The tense silence in the car was broken only by Colletti, who mumbled curses at the traffic and other drivers as he expertly maneuvered his way through the city streets. Stein sat shotgun and was quiet, serious, and pensive. Keane sat behind Stein and did his best to relax.

Over the years he had developed a methodical sense of calm whenever he was to enter into a new case, or a serious situation. He knew he wanted no distractions. He didn't want to think about his mother, or his failed marriage, or his young daughter who had just started her first year of college. He needed emptiness. So he shut off his thoughts and stared out at nothing.

Chapter Five

8:33 am / East 93rd Street, Our Lady of Perpetual Hope School For Girls

When they arrived at 93rd Street, patrol had everything blocked off from both ends of the street. Colletti threw the car in park and jumped out, slammed the driver's side door shut and rushed up to meet with Sergeant Diaz of the 21st Precinct. Diaz had taken charge of the scene at the rectory and the block surrounding it. He was a slim, dark-skinned man with jet black hair that he wore slicked straight back.

"What you got for us, Sergeant Diaz?" Colletti asked.

"They killed a nun... It's fucking bad man, the worst I've ever seen."

"Fuck," Colletti whispered.

Stein and Keane approached the pair simultaneously, both with their notepads in their hands.

"What do we got?" asked Stein.

"One of the nuns has been killed," Colletti reported. "Sergeant Diaz says it's the worst he's ever seen."

Diaz greeted Stein and Keane solemnly, and then nodded towards the building and said, "Come on, I'll show ya."

Stein turned to Jimmy Colletti, "Jimmy, take note of everyone who shows from the adjoining squads, the Commissioner's or Mayor's Office, Homicide Task Force, etcetera. You know what to do, collect everyone's names and anything we'll need for the Unusual report please."

"You got it," Colletti replied.

The all-girls school of Our Lady of Perpetual Hope stood in the middle of the block, surrounded by brownstones and pre-war buildings. The pale stone structure, which was completed in 1892, rose above the street with crenellated bricks and turrets and large arched windows. The black wrought iron gates were open and an officer in uniform stood ashen-faced on the stairs leading up to the entrance.

Keane and the officer locked eyes for a moment before Tommy looked away, shaking his head slightly to clear away the man's obvious apprehension and to ease his own nerves. He didn't want any emotions or preconceived ideas before seeing the scene himself.

The four men continued toward the rectory, Stein rattling off questions towards Sergeant Diaz as they walked.

"This place has been on total lockdown since the first officers on the scene, right? No one in here, to your knowledge, other than first responding officers and yourself? Who called the police? Did that person discover the body? And you guys have kept everyone out of the crime scene, yes?"

Diaz answered everything as best he could. As far as he knew it was a clean crime scene, and the officers first on the scene, David Cone and Alicia Fernandez, had done nothing more than step into the room where the homicide had taken place, step back out and close the door.

The scene of the crime was the office belonging to the victim, Sister Margaret. No one, other than the two first responders, Sergeant Diaz and his driver, Officer Holt, and Sister Elizabeth, the nun who discovered the body, were known to have been inside the room. All of this had occurred within the last thirty to forty minutes.

The four of them reached the closed office door, and Stein spoke.

"Colletti, you and Sergeant Diaz collect everyone who is here now who has anything to do with this building, this school, and put them somewhere and tell them not to leave. If you got someone available from patrol, have them baby-sit them and instruct them not to talk about the case until we have a chance to interview them. When the Lu and Doyle arrive, you and Doyle go record all the license plates up and down the street and around the block for a two-block radius. Also call the Medical Examiner and the Crime Scene Unit, tell them we got a homicide.

"They're on their way. I already made the call," Sergeant Diaz interjected.

"Great, thank you Sergeant. See if we can get some more patrol up here to keep everyone, especially the press, off this block. Keane, you wanna add anything?"

"Keep goin, you're on a roll," Tommy replied as he slowly opened the door and stepped into the room.

He could hear Lieutenant Bricks and Doyle arrive behind him, but their voices started to fade as Tommy took in everything in the room. "Fuck me," he heard Lieutenant Bricks exclaim followed by an "Oh my God" from Doyle.

Sister Margaret

Tommy stopped in front of Sister Margaret's large oak desk and stared. Stein, about a foot behind him and to the right, did the same. They silently looked upon the body of Sister Margaret, a nun, an educator, and the principal of the all-girls academy of Our Lady of Perpetual Hope, grades six through twelve.

Tommy had seen some brutal and horrific homicides during his nineteen years, but this one ranked up towards the top. He allowed himself to feel a moment of pity and grief for the life lost before him before he mentally shook his head clear and detached himself. He needed to see her and this room with no feeling.

Sister Margaret was sitting back in a large, black leather office chair. Her head was tilted back against the chair, her blue eyes open wide and staring up at the ceiling with a tight grimace frozen upon her thin lips. She was half naked. Her habit was pulled up and tucked into the neckline of the garment to hold it up and expose her naked bottom half. Her thin legs were spread apart to expose her vagina, her clunky black shoes and white socks were still on. She had no bra on and her panties were crumpled around her left ankle.

Sister Margaret's torso was cut open from about two inches above her crotch to midway up her sternum, then again side to side just below her belly button. There was a large, stainless steel kitchen knife plunged, almost up to its handle, approximately where her heart would be.

Her wounds were so deep that the edges of the cuts curled outward, exposing Sister Margaret's layers of skin, the yellow layer of fat, and then the deep maroons of the muscle tissue. The blues and grays of her entrails appeared to be wanting to fall from her body onto the tiled floor.

Keane spoke without turning from the body. "Lu, I want you, Doyle, and Colletti to come in here and stand where

I am standing. I want you all to take in everything you can from this room. Once Crime Scene is done and the body is gone we won't be able to do this again. Don't touch anything, hands in your pockets, and just take it all in. Take as long as you need then leave the room for me and Stein, please."

Tommy backed out of the room and tapped Stein on the shoulder to join him.

"And do me a favor--don't discuss what you see amongst yourselves, or with anyone else, until Stein and I speak to each of you first."

As Keane and Stein stepped outside of the small office, Captain Joseph Peleggi came storming down the hall, with his driver hurrying after him. His coat was open, and it flapped behind him in his haste as he came and stood in front of both detectives and put his hands on his hips.

"What do we have here, Detectives? I understand a nun has been murdered?"

"Yes sir," replied Stein.

"In here?" The Captain asked and stepped toward the office door. Tommy put his hand up, stopping Captain Peleggi in his tracks.

"Please sir, there's no need for you to enter the crime scene."

Peleggi looked at Stein in disbelief. "What do you mean, Detective?" he scoffed. "This is my precinct and *my* crime scene."

"With all due respect, Captain, this is our crime scene and we would very much like to keep it as clean as possible before all the evidence collection has been done. Please, Captain, there is no need for you to enter the room."

Joseph Peleggi huffed and pushed Keane's hand away as he stepped into the room.

"Oh my God," he exclaimed, almost as though he was sorry he hadn't listened to Keane.

He stepped back out, his face pale, and without looking at either detective he turned and started to walk back down the hall. "This will be a press case, Detectives," he called out. "Do a good job and don't fuck it up. Find whatever evil scumbag did this, and find him fast."

Hours went by, as they do at any homicide: waiting for the Crime Scene and Evidence Collection Units to show up, waiting for them to take all their measurements and photographs, to take blood samples, fiber samples, fingerprints, and the like.

Then more waiting, this time for the Medical Examiner to arrive and pronounce the body officially dead, and then to deliver a cause of death. Then it was again Keane and Stein's turn in the room, poking around until they finally okayed the transport of the corpse to the morgue by the Medical Examiner's office for an autopsy and further forensics.

Doyle and Colletti had done preliminary interviews of many of the school's staff and collected the names and contact information for anyone present who was affiliated with the school in anyway. Stein and Keane poured over the body and the office, they interviewed the Monseigneur, Father Busto, Sister Elizabeth, the head janitor, Ed Steely, and his assistant, Pedro Fuentes--all were shocked.

They each asked who could have committed such an evil act and who would have had access to the school so early in the morning. On the surface, no one had any information that seemed relevant or that seemed to point in any meaningful direction.

Hours later, the team converged in the hallway in front of Sister Margaret's office. Each looked worse for wear, with the stress and strain of the day showing on their faces. Stein spoke to the group as he leaned back against the wall.

"Listen, I know it's late and we've been here for hours, but we have hours more to go. Doreen and Jimmy, please canvas a two block perimeter and see what you can get as far as surveillance cameras go. Hopefully someone, somewhere, caught whoever this animal is walking past and we have him on film. Tommy, lets you and I get together on this now and go over our thoughts and all these interviews, see what we can come up with."

"Sounds good. Let's start at the diner though, I'm fucking starving. We can all meet up at the House after." Tommy rubbed his face with both hands, trying to shake off some of the fatigue.

"Sounds good," Doyle replied.

"Roger that," Colletti chimed in.

As they all left the school, they could see reporters, at least a dozen of them, waiting at the corner. Doyle and Colletti broke off from the group and headed across the street, while Stein and Keane headed towards the corner.

"A press case," Tommy mumbled.

"Get used to it. Half the shit that happens in this precinct is a press case," Stein snorted. "Ten blocks north of here and some poor Puerto Rican or Black girl gets raped and murdered, they won't even put a blurb on page ten about it. But some asshole down here grabs five asses in one night? Shit, the front page headline will be 'Upper East Side Groper on the Loose.' That's the way it is here, it's what sells papers and gets you to tune into your television. That being said, not for nothing but a Catholic School nun being fucking cut in half in her own office before class... I'd consider that a press case."

"I'm not in disagreement," replied Keane as they simultaneously began repeating; 'No comment. No comment'; to the questions being yelled at them by the waiting press.

Chapter Six

Keane and Stein parked their sedan outside of the diner on 86th Street, in the bus stop. They pushed open the glass door and were greeted by the host: an older, balding Greek man, dressed in the customary black pants, white shirt, and black vest typical of a diner uniform.

He brought them to an open booth in the rear of the restaurant, just past the bank of windows overlooking the street.

Another older Greek man, nearly identical albeit with more hair, set down two glasses of water and took their order. Tommy ordered a turkey club and Stein a Yankee bean soup and pastrami on rye with mustard.

As soon as the waiter walked away with their order, a young, clean-cut Puerto Rican man in a grey sport coat and tie approached their booth.

"Excuse me, Detectives? I'm Gil Nunez from the Daily--"

"Are you fucking kidding me?" Tommy interrupted, "Can't you see we're sitting down to eat? If you know who we are and what we've been doing all day, you'd think you'd have a little fucking courtesy."

"But, I just want to-- I think the people--"

"Fuck the people and fuck you," Tommy jabbed a finger in the reporter's direction. "Now get away from our table or the headline you'll be writing will be about a hot-headed detective kicking the shit out of an impolite reporter. Go on... Fuck off."

Stein looked up at the young reporter, over the rim of his glasses, and smiled. "I'd do what he says son. He's got a reputation as a hard, hard fucker and I wouldn't put it past him to kick the living shit out of you over a turkey sandwich."

Gil Nunez stood up straight and replied as he stepped backwards away from the booth. "I'm sorry gentlemen, I really am." He then turned and promptly exited the diner.

Stein and Keane looked at each other and both laughed at the reporter's departure. The waiter brought out their meals and they sobered up and discussed the homicide at length as they ate, Stein looking over the top of his glasses at Keane like a school teacher.

During their discussion, they discovered that they had both, separately, come to the same conclusion. There was no sign of theft, no sign of forced entry, and although Sister Margaret was mostly naked and there seemed to be an underlying sexual deviance to the crime, she didn't appear to have been raped, a fact that the Medical Examiner also mentioned after her initial examination at the scene. Nor did it seem she put up much of a fight, if any at all.

The cause of her death seemed obvious and the knife in her chest was most likely the only murder weapon used. So barring any new or unusual evidence found by the Medical

Examiner or the forensics lab, they came to the same immediate conclusion--the murder of Sister Margaret was a fairly passionate crime of hate.

Whether it was committed directly against Sister Margaret or towards the Church as a whole was a distinction to be made, but both detectives leaned towards the former--that it was aimed at the Sister herself. Both took note however, that the way she was cut open from top to bottom in a singular line and then from side to side on the lower portion of her torso, also in a singular line, formed an upside down cross, making the latter scenario seem like a possibility.

As they finished their dinner and leaned back away from their plates, Stein pushed his glasses up his nose and regarded Keane.

"I like the way you think, Tommy."

"You ain't a bad thinker yourself there, Detective, and it was nice to meet you today." Tommy smiled at Stein and then signaled for the check. "Tonight's on me, Stein."

The waiter approached and instead of the check handed Tommy a business card. "A young man paid your check and asked that I give this to you."

The business card was from Gilberto Nunez and on the back he had written, 'So sorry to have interrupted your meal, I meant no disrespect. ~Gil'

"What do you know, the kid's a class act," Tommy exclaimed.

"Maybe you taught him a lesson, Tommy."

***

Stein and Keane climbed the stairs up to the squad room of the 2-1 where the rest of the team was converged. They were now in their fifteenth hour on the job, and each of them looked it. They took turns offering what they had so far on the case. Colletti and Doyle had several hours of video that they had retrieved from a number of different locations, and more promised to be delivered the next day.

They had run searches of all of the license plate numbers from the block, had a long list of names and addresses of people who worked for the school, who worked and lived on the block, and of anyone who was anywhere in that vicinity from a few hours before the crime to a few hours after the crime. This was the tedious part of detective work, since 99.9% of this was certain to prove unfruitful. But, to search continually and leave no stone unturned until the truth is found--this is the nature of detective work.

Stein and Keane took the other squad members into the Lieutenant's office one at a time so Keane could ask each of them his one question: "What did you see at the crime scene?"

Lieutenant Bricks was the first to join them, and as a seasoned investigator himself, he essentially restated the synopsis of Keane and Stein's own private conversation. He thought the murder was a brutal, hateful act and was either committed against Sister Margaret personally, or was an act against the Church itself. The big question for the Lieutenant centered around the lack of obvious resistance by Sister Margaret, and, if there had been any sexual contact, it was not notably visible to the investigators or the Medical Examiner.

Detective Colletti was called in next and his insight was simple and obvious.

"Whatever sick mother fucker could cut up a nun like that is an evil sick fuck... An upside down cross? That is some fucked up satanic shit right there... some kinda Charles Manson cult shit," he said as he ran his fingers through his hair.

"What else did you see, Jimmy?" Keane asked.

"I don't know. I mean, I saw an innocent nun cut in half by some sadistic fucking psycho, that's what I saw."

"Okay Jimmy, we got that, listen... keep that picture in your head. Keep it in your head and if anything unusual comes to mind let us know what it is, no matter how small," Keane replied. Then, "Send Doyle in please."

"Keep it in my mind?" Colletti said as he stood up from the chair and looked at both Stein, who was leaning against the wall with his shoulder, and Keane who sat at the Lieutenant's desk, "How the fuck am I ever gonna get that sick shit *out* of my mind?"

Doyle entered the room next and took the chair just vacated by Jimmy.

"Hey Doreen, how you doing? It's a long one today and you've done great so far, thanks. I want to ask you simply, what did you see at the crime scene?"

Doreen looked down and took a deep breath, not making eye contact with either Keane or Stein, and let it out with a sigh.

"I saw a brutal murder," she said, and paused. "I believe this was most certainly a murder of passion and hate." She paused again. "I think whoever did this planned to do it and not only wanted to kill Sister Margaret, but also wanted to send a message."

She paused a little longer.

"Go on, just keep going," Detective Keane said.

"I think this was definitely someone who knew and who hated Sister Margaret. I also think the way they left her, with her legs spread and the upside down cross cut into her body, they wanted to make a statement. I don't imagine it to be satanic or cult-driven--I know that's what Jimmy thinks. But I think this is something personal... maybe against the Church and taken out on Sister Margaret, I think that's possible, that's still a possibility... but I really feel whoever did this knew and hated Sister Margaret herself and wanted to make or *prove* some sort of point. He wanted to make a statement, he wanted to embarrass and humiliate her in death..."

Doyle sighed again, and continued, "I don't see any sex here. Yes, on the surface all the nudity looks sexual, but I didn't see anything to me that said rape or sodomy. And it's been nagging at me--I didn't notice anything about Sister Margaret that showed any fight, and nothing in the room indicated that either... but there she was, displayed and cut up that way. She was a nun, would she be that passive to willingly allow this to happen? Is that possible? None of the Sisters at my school would have endured that without a fight, I know that. And I also think? Once we find the guy who did this, it's gonna be a strange fucking story."

"Thanks, Doreen. That's exactly what I wanted," Keane replied.

"That's it?" asked Doyle.

"Yeah, go home and get some sleep. We're gonna have a long day again tomorrow."

"Okay, Tommy, Mark, I'll see youse in the morning."

"Nice job, Doyle," Stein remarked.

"Thanks. Goodnight guys."

Doyle walked out of the room and gently shut the door behind her. Mark Stein pushed off of the wall and took the chair facing the desk. Tommy leaned back in his chair.

"So what you think? You heard what they all had to say."

Stein replied, "Well the Lu is right there with us. Jimmy, fucking Jimmy is a little emotional here. I don't think it's a cult of crazed Satanists, but this is something personal. There's something we are not yet seeing, not on the face of things... yeah it's brutal, and it's hateful. I don't like to use sick or psychotic...I don't think those words help an investigation, any investigation process move forward--but I think we are all onto something... that there is some level of hate towards both Sister Margaret and the Catholic Church. I also don't see a sexual link here other than humiliation, but we'll have to see what we get back from the lab on that. It's way too soon to tell but there is something there and we're gonna find out what it is."

"Okay," Tommy replied, "But there is one thing... one sex thing that no one has pointed out yet, and I don't know if you noticed it. I didn't mention it at meal because I wanted to see who else noticed it."

"What is it?" asked Stein.

"Get that picture of Sister Margaret in your mind, Stein, and tell me why would a nun shave her pussy? No one has asked that, her pubic growth looked like a man who hasn't shaved in two days. What was it? Maybe an eighth of an inch long, if that? What nun shaves her pussy? There's certainly nothing illegal or immoral there--cleanliness is next to godliness they say--but it don't make sense, Stein, and no one noticed it."

"Hmmm, you may be onto something here. You know I'm a Jew, my wife hasn't even trimmed since our Honeymoon.

The thing is like a broccoli patch down there. Fuck, you think that would have been the first thing I noticed. This is interesting, Keane... Good eye, but please don't keep any more secret observations to yourself."

"Hey, I will keep nothing from you, Stein. I just wanted to listen to everyone else's insights first. I got a method, a process... It sort of helps me unravel this shit."

"Yes I see that, and it's quite interesting. Tomorrow," Stein said as he stood up.

"Yeah, I'll see you tomorrow morning," Tommy replied.

"First stop the morgue to see what the autopsy revealed."

"Yes sir. Goodnight."

Tommy and the rest of B-Squad had completed an eighteen-hour shift with no definitive leads.

Chapter Seven

Tommy woke, in his pitch black room, sixty-two minutes before his alarm was set to ring. He dropped down and did his fifty push-ups in complete darkness, thinking only of the details of the prior day's crime scene: Sister Margaret's face staring up at the ceiling, the way she was posed, naked and gutted for all to see.

He knew everything was a clue, everything in that room had meaning--he just had to find out what it was. Tommy thought of the dozens of different fingerprints Crime Scene would have lifted--this was a school after all.

How many people entered and left that office every day?

'Best we could hope for is a usable print on the knife,' Tommy thought. 'That would be great.' What would the Medical Examiner be able to add? The cause of death was obvious, but certainly there was a piece or two of the puzzle waiting with the ME's office.

"Okay," Tommy said to himself in the dark. "Clear it all, empty your brain, get it all out and start fresh." He turned on the bedroom lights and headed to the bathroom for a shower and a shave.

Sister Margaret

"Good morning, Tommy," his mother called from the living room as soon as he opened his door. "You were home late last night, Tommy. I waited up till after midnight but I couldn't stay awake for you Tommy... Tommy? Were you looking for that evil man who killed the nun Tommy? It's on the TV this morning Tommy, every channel. Tommy, every channel has the nun on it...That's where you were, weren't you Tommy? Chasing after that nun's killer, weren't you? Were you, Tommy?"

"Morning Ma," Tommy called back from the hall." Yes, that's where I was all day yesterday, chasing that nun's killer."

Tommy walked over and gave her a kiss on the top of her head as she sat in her recliner. She was wearing her purple flannel nightgown that he had bought her the previous Mother's Day. A cigarette was smoldering in the ashtray.

"Well good for them they brought you down here for this one, Tommy. If anyone can catch that evil bastard, it's my Tommy. Was it a bad one? It sounds like it was a bad one on the TV... Was it a bad one Tommy?"

"Yeah Ma, it was a bad one."

"Well it's good for them they have you on this case, Tommy. If anyone can catch this..."

"We'll get him Ma. I promise we'll find out who did this and bring him in."

"I know you will Tommy, if anyone can my Tommy can. Do you want something to eat Tommy? Can I make you some breakfast, Tommy?"

"No Ma, I'm gonna shower and go, okay? I got a bad guy to catch."

"Yes, so don't waste time here Tommy. Get something to eat at the precinct and then go find this animal, Tommy."

Tommy showered, shaved, dressed, and headed out the door, kissing his mother on his way past her as she stared at the television set, still watching the news. Tommy intentionally tuned out the reporter's voice as he crossed the room.

He stepped out onto the front stoop of the building and scanned the block up and down.

He braced himself slightly against the wind--it was unusually cold for an October morning. Then he buttoned up the front of his leather car coat and started to walk to work. On the way he intentionally cleared his mind of all thoughts and breathed in deeply, feeling the cool air fill his lungs.

As he turned the corner onto the block of the 2-1, he saw news vans and reporters outside, no doubt waiting for an interview, for something they could spin into a story. Tommy crossed the street to try and avoid contact. He came up from behind the group of reporters and cut right through the crowd and they never saw him coming until he was already inside the door.

He was an hour early for his scheduled shift and as he entered the squad room he found Stein already at his desk. "Good morning," both men simultaneously announced to each other.

"Good to see you in so early." Stein said as Tommy sat down in the chair at Doyle's desk, directly across from him.

"So, what you got? Or what do you think? Anything?" asked Tommy.

"No, nothing. Nothing yet anyways," Stein replied. "We have photos and some other stuff from Crime Scene back but nothing is helping me yet... Nothing back from the prints yet either." Stein adjusted his glasses. "I've been thinking about this all night, going over the interviews, but right now, I have nothing, Tom. You want to head down to the morgue with me and see what the ME has for us?"

"Yeah, let's go. I'm curious what they'll have to add."

Both detectives left the precinct, leaving a note for the others to request an immediate call with any new information.

***

The city morgue was located at Bellevue Hospital--a nondescript building of pale cement, the exterior of which belied the sinister, dark interior. Keane and Stein walked down the hallway conscious of the faint smell of disinfectant and decay that lingered in the air. They stopped at the desk and introduced themselves to the young Hispanic man.

They were happy to find out that not only was the preliminary report on Sister Margaret completed, but also that the Medical Examiner who wrote it, the one they met at the crime scene, was still in the building.

The man at the desk picked up the phone and quietly spoke into it. He hung up and nodded at the detectives. Within a few minutes, Kristen Smyth, a young woman of about thirty, came out from an autopsy room and walked toward them. With freckles and honey blonde hair cut in a bob, she looked more like a kindergarten teacher than a Medical Examiner who dug through dead bodies and visited crime scenes.

Smyth greeted each detective with a handshake. "Nice to see you gentlemen again. I'm so glad you made it down here so early," she said, then gestured toward the room where Sister Margaret's body was being kept.

"Basically, there isn't much more to it than what I mentioned at the scene yesterday," Smyth explained as she walked them through her findings. "There are no signs of any kind of struggle on the body. Lack of lividity would suggest the body was dead for no more than ninety minutes before you were on the scene. Your victim was stabbed in the heart first-- this killed her almost instantly. She was then mutilated, cut first across the body's lower midsection from her left side to her right and then from the bottom, midway between her navel and her vagina, to the top. Your attacker cut deep until he hit the sternum and then the next two inches just cut through the flesh. He used his right hand and a common chef's knife with an eight inch blade. Once he finished with the cross cut and upward cut, he stabbed her in the heart a second time. The first wound, though, I believe is the one that killed her; if she were alive through the whole ordeal her heart would have pumped out considerably more blood."

She pushed her hair behind her ears and looked up for a moment, running it all through her mind again.

"Other than that, I really don't have much. Since she was seated, I don't have any read on the attacker's height or size, and as of right now we have nothing back from the toxicology tests yet. You two may examine the body here as long as you need to, and of course ask any questions, but other than that... I don't have much else for you."

"Yeah, I kinda thought as much... as far as her being dead before she was mutilated," Tommy replied. "Here is a question, Kristen, an odd one but one that is gnawing at us... do you find it unusual for a nun to have shaved her pubic area?"

"I don't find many things to be strange, Detective, and nowadays I find more women than less do shave or trim their pubic area, but yes I do find it interesting being that she is a nun. Nonetheless I assume it was what she preferred… You guys have any leads yet?" Smyth asked.

"Nothing yet," Stein replied, "nothing yet."

"Well, good luck. Catch this fuck head," she said with a tone that no kindergarten teacher would use. "Lab results should be to you in the next day or two."

"That's the plan, and thanks," Stein replied.

The detectives left the morgue and started down the sidewalk toward the car.

"So our guy is right-handed and killed the Sister before he sliced her up," Stein said as he thought out loud.

Just then his phone started to vibrate with a text message. He looked down and read the text from Jimmy Colletti aloud to Tommy: "Bingo! I think we have something on video. Come back ASAP to check it out, you'll be happy!'"

"Awesome. Let's go," replied Tommy, and they hurried to the car.

***

Upon returning to the Station House, Keane and Stein were greeted by Colletti, Doyle, Lieutenant Bricks, and Sergeant Browne. They were all in the main detective area near the cage, all with smiles on their faces and hope in their eyes.

Immediately Jimmy Colletti began to speak in an excited manner, "We found him, Mark! I think we got your guy on video at four locations and I think you know him."

"Really? That's great, Jimmy. What did you find?"

"Okay, well we went over all the video we could find yesterday, last night, and this morning and at the approximate time we believe the homicide occurred, we found this guy passing two cameras heading toward the school. And then the same two heading back from the school exactly sixteen minutes later. Doreen went and walked it just a little while ago and it all adds up. He woulda had exactly enough time to get to the school, spend six minutes killing the nun and then pass these cameras the second time."

"Really... Good work, excellent work," said Stein.

"But wait," Jimmy continued, "It gets better, we think we know the guy... and if we're right, you locked him up yourself last year--"

"Huh? Who do you think it is?" Stein interrupted.

Jimmy continued, "Do you remember a skinny little junkie by the name of Benjamin Hirschle? That little fuck you pinched for fighting with the priest over at Saint Dominic's on 85th, the guy who was stealing bibles, and breaking into the poor boxes? What did he have? Like five open Complaint Reports on him for that shit?"

"Wow. Benjamin Hirschle... yeah the one that Father Sinissi beat the balls off of when he caught him forcing open the poor box. Four bibles tucked under his jacket! Wow... so he may be our boy then? Well, let's go pick him up."

"Last known address is where he lived last year when you locked him up, Mark," Sergeant Browne reported, "427 East 83rd Street. Apartment 4FW."

The detectives all stood up, grabbed their jackets, and headed toward the door.

"Hey..." Lieutenant Bricks called after them, "be careful with this guy. All four of you go over there and be smart. No hero shit, and if you need back up, or ESU, call for it."

Sister Margaret

***

3:12 pm / 427 East 83rd Street

Doreen and Jimmy set up across the street, by a blue car, where they could keep an eye on the windows and the fire escape on the fourth floor. They also had a visual of the roof and up and down the block. Tommy and Stein would enter the building to see if they could catch Hirschle at home. "Put one of your radios on point to point," Stein told the others, and then looked at his partner, "You ready, Tommy?"

"Yup. Let's go."

The two detectives entered the building's vestibule and rang all four first floor apartment bells. A few moments later there was a garbled sound over the intercom as two or more people answered the rings, then someone buzzed the door open.

Both detectives immediately headed up the stairs, bypassing the first floor apartments. 427 was an old ten-family tenement building that had been renovated into a very nice twenty-family building, by cutting all the old two-bedroom apartments down to small one-bedrooms and studios.

They reached the fourth floor and, without speaking, positioned themselves side-by-side along the wall beside the door that read 4FW, their pistols drawn. Tommy knocked on the door three times... then three times more... then again.

"Hello?" A female voice answered, "Hello, who's there?"

"It's the police. We're detectives from the 21st Precinct. Please open up ma'am," Stein replied.

"Police?" The voice responded, "Can you put your ID to the peephole, please?"

Tommy raised his shield to the small circle on the door.

"Okay." The three locks tumbled and clanked open and a small, dark-haired, attractive woman of about forty years cracked open the door. "Hello...What happened, what do you want from me?" she asked, without opening the door more than four inches.

"We're looking for Benny, Miss," Stein replied.

"Benny? You mean Benjamin Hirschle? He doesn't live here anymore. He lived here before I moved in over a year ago... I still get his mail sometimes."

"Okay, Miss. May we still come in and check?" asked Tommy.

"I don't know... Do you have a warrant?"

"No we don't have a warrant, Miss, and we don't need one if you say yes. We just need to ask you a couple of questions and make certain that Benny doesn't live here anymore. You're not in any sort of trouble, Miss," Stein replied.

"Questions? For what? I don't know anything."

"Well, you still may be able to help us. Please, it's important and will only take a minute," said Stein.

"Okay... I guess it's okay."

Stein thanked the woman as he and Tommy stepped into her apartment. It was small, stylish, and neat. They stood in the main room, which was a small kitchenette and living room.

Stein asked her to sit down on the sofa and she grabbed a throw pillow as she sat and put it in her lap, as if for protection. Tommy made his way to an adjoining room with an open door and stuck his head in. It was a small room, approximately ten by twelve with a double bed centered against the far wall and a few pieces of pine furniture, also neat and stylish.

"What is he looking for?" the woman asked, craning her neck to look around Stein.

"Listen, we are looking for Benny Hirschle, and it is very important we find him. Can you help us out? Have you seen him at all recently?" asked Stein.

"No, I told you. I moved here about a year ago. I've never met Mr. Hirschle. This wasn't even his apartment, it belonged to a girl named Sharon Stiles... I sometimes get mail for the both of them, but no I don't know anything about them. From what I've heard from other neighbors, they were not good people... I assume that's why you're looking for them, or him, but I'm sorry. I don't know anything else. Maybe the super can help you? She lives on the first floor in 1RE."

Tommy stepped into the room after checking out the bathroom and shook his head no--there was no one in the apartment but the three of them.

"Okay, Miss, thank you so much. We're sorry to have bothered you and we appreciate your time," Stein said.

"Yes, we appreciate you talking to us. You helped us out more than you may think," Tommy added as they stepped to the front door and opened it.

"Well, you're welcome... Sorry I couldn't help more," the woman said as they stepped out and she closed the door.

Tommy and Stein made their way down the narrow stairs to the first floor and walked toward the back of the building where they knocked on the supers' door at apartment 1RE.

A stout, grey-haired Scottish woman, wearing an oversized corduroy button-down shirt and jeans, answered the door almost immediately and in a deep Scottish accent demanded, "Are ye da ones that were a ringen me bell a moment ago? ...Da police are ye? Ye look like police ta me."

Tommy smiled. "Yes ma'am, I'm Detective Keane and this is Detective Stein. We're looking for a Benny Hirschle who lived up in 4FW."

"Nahhh you'lla find no Benny Hirschle here. That piece of shite was arrested for fighten a priest bout a year and a half ago... never came back, and we evicted his shite lady friend Sharon bout da same time. Fucken shites da both of dem. Whadaya want wit him? Drugs I bet... They was both fiends I know it."

Her eyes widened briefly and then she squinted at them. "Nahh... nahh don't tell me it's dat nun, he was fighten priests and now he's killen nuns... nahhh dats too much. But I wouldn't put it past him. He's a wee skinny fella, but a desperate little shite he is."

"No no, ma'am... We just need to talk to him. Do you know where he may be living now?" asked Stein.

"He left here for Rikers but I know he's out. I've seen him twice, once on 86th Street wit dat Sharon and another time sleepin on a bench in Carl Schurz Park near da Peter Pan. Ooohhh yer not tellin me are youse? It's dat nun, innit? He done dat nun, dat piece a shite, dint 'e?"

"No ma'am, we just have a few questions for him. But please, don't tell anyone we were looking for him, okay? And if you hear anything, anything at all, please call us here." Stein handed her a business card.

"Okay, lovies. You best bet I will," she said as she closed and locked the door.

Chapter Eight

The detectives stepped out onto the stoop of the building, shaking their heads to Doyle and Colletti across the street. Although they didn't find Benny, they now were fairly certain, with the super's confirmation that she had seen him in the neighborhood, that he may be the man they saw in the video. And with this possibility, they believed he could be the perpetrator.

Stein and Keane decided to head up to Saint Dominic's to see Father Sinissi while Doyle and Colletti returned to the squad room to follow up on any new leads and hunt down Hirschle and his girlfriend, Sharon Stiles.

At Saint Dominic's, they found Father Sinissi in the office of the rectory. He was about fifty-five years old, a handsome man with a receding hairline and a strong athletic build that was evident even through his un-tailored priest garments. He was sitting behind a battered wooden desk, looking over some papers, when Stein tapped on the door frame.

"Detective Mark Stein," Father Sinissi greeted them with a broad smile, "Welcome, welcome." He stood up and made his way around his desk to shake Stein's hand.

"Father Sinissi, this is Detective Tom Keane," said Stein.

"Detective Keane. I believe I have heard of you, Detective. You have quite the reputation amongst the men in blue I understand. It is very nice to meet you." He leaned toward Tommy and firmly shook his hand. "I am afraid to ask why the visit, Detectives. Am I wrong to assume it has to do with dear Sister Margaret?"

"Yes Father, I'm sorry to say that it does. We are working the case and have some questions we'd like to ask," Tommy replied.

"Please, please by all means come in and sit down," Father Sinissi gestured to a comfortable loveseat and two wingback chairs nestled in the corner of his office. "Can I get either of you something to drink? Some coffee or tea? Water?"

"No, thank you, Father," Stein replied, sitting down. "We want to ask you if you have seen, or if there is anything you can tell us about your old friend Benjamin Hirschle."

"Benjamin Hirschle... I have seen him, yes. Three or four times in the neighborhood, once he was so high he could barely stand up, just kept swaying back and forth. Other times just walking down the street. We made eye contact once but I don't think he even knew who I was," Father Sinissi stated.

"And how well did you know Sister Margaret, Father?" Tommy asked.

"Oh, I knew her very well," he replied with a sigh. "She has done wonderful work with the girls in her school and has been with the Diocese for many years. She is--was--a wonderful hard worker, even an overachiever, if it is possible to over achieve when doing God's work, I don't know. So you think Benjamin committed this terrible crime? I can only assume so, he does have a history of crimes against our Church...You think it was him, don't you?"

"We have our suspicions, Father. Do you have any idea where Benny may be living now?" Tommy asked, "Have you, or anyone else, seen him here at Saint Dominic's or any other church? Please take a moment and think, it's very important that we find him soon."

Father Sinissi leaned back in his chair and thought for a moment. Then he slowly shook his head. "Other than the few times I have seen him on the street, I haven't seen nor heard anything of Benjamin Hirschle. I will certainly do my best to find out for you gentlemen though."

"Well be cool, Father, we don't want him running because he knows we are looking for him. We also don't want you, or any of your staff or parishioners, putting themselves in harm's way. But yes, please keep an open ear and let us know what you hear," Tommy added.

"You'll find I am as cool as they come, Detective, and I understand--we will leave the police work to the police."

"Now, can you think of any reason why anyone else would do something like this to Sister Margaret? Anyone who would want to hurt her for any reason, or anyone else who had something against the Church or the school?" asked Tommy.

Father Sinissi frowned and leaned forward, putting his forearms on his knees. "I thought you had your man, Detective? Are you not searching for Benjamin Hirschle for this crime?"

"Yes, Father, he is a person of interest to us but we don't want to miss out on any information leading us to the killer, if in fact Benny is the wrong man," Tommy answered.

Sister Margaret

"Ahhh, yes of course I understand," Father Sinissi leaned back once again into the wing chair, and said, "No. Immediately no one comes to mind. It's really a quiet neighborhood. Some of our parishioners' children attend Our Lady of Perpetual Hope, and all are happy there. It's a very good school... I know there are many lunatics these days, and terrorists are a new worry, but we have never had threats made to this church of any sort. To my knowledge, I have heard nothing hateful towards any of the other churches in the area either, and nothing towards Our Lady of Perpetual Hope... not ever. Benjamin Hirschle is the only one I can think of, and even then I would not have guessed him capable of such an act. Yet here you are, asking me about him, so I assume you may know something more than just my personal history with him."

"No Father, we are just... searching for the answers. Looking for clues to a mystery," Tommy replied with a sigh.

Chapter Nine

The two detectives stepped out of the rectory and stood on the sidewalk.

"What next?" Tommy asked Stein.

"Let me message Doreen and see what they have over there, if anything." Stein pulled out his cell and sent a text while Tommy looked up and down the block. A few minutes later, Stein's phone buzzed.

"Doreen says they have an address for Sharon Stiles: 155 East 103rd. Let's go check it out."

Stein pulled their car up to the address. The time was now 7:25 pm. The sun had set and the street was quiet. People were already tucked away in their apartments after the workday and the commute home. The only person out was an older woman, wrapped up in a scarf and an old threadbare coat, walking her beagle.

Stein and Keane exited the car and scanned their surroundings. They entered the building's vestibule and found the name on the bell; Stiles 3B. The second door leading into the building had no lock in the cylinder and the detectives proceeded in. They were met in the hallway by an older black man, approximately sixty-five years old, with grey dreadlocks and an army green knit cap.

Sister Margaret

"Hey DT's... who you looking for?"

"Yup, you got us. Detective Stein, 21st Squad and we're looking for Sharon Stiles. You know her?"

"Hells yeah I do. That crazy white girl lives on three. You after her for drugs or is her daddy after her dirty ass to bring her back home, where it shoulda stayed?" the man replied.

"Have you seen her? Do you know if she's home? How about her boyfriend? Has he been around lately?" asked Stein.

"She has a few boyfriends, if you want to call them that, but you are probably asking about skinny Benny. That one, he's in and outta here all the time. He a crazy junkie, too! I catch him sleeping in the hall sometimes at the top of the stairs by the roof."

"Are you the super here?" asked Stein.

"I'm like half a super, I help with the trash and do a little cleaning. I don't fix nothing though... Hey, if you're after those two, do us all a solid and get them outta here. This neighborhood's been getting better. We got no more Puerto Rican junkies in the building or on this block, and we don't need any new little white junkies movin in just cause they be paying more rent than the Puerto Ricans." He moved aside and gestured for them to proceed up the stairs. "Go to 3B, that's where they stayin, the both of them. Don't know if either is home. I ain't seen neither all day."

"Thank you sir, we appreciate the help," said Tommy.

"Okay DT's, I'm happy to help. I'm pro-Police--I like to know you're cleaning up the neighborhood."

Tommy and Stein climbed the steps to the third floor and approached the door. There was music playing from inside and Tommy put his ear to the door. He heard a woman's voice and nodded to Stein. They both drew their weapons and Tommy knocked on the door. Tap. Tap. Tap. A female voice answered.

"Who is it?"

"It's the plumber ma'am. There's a leak in the apartment downstairs and we think it's coming from your bathroom," Tommy replied.

"Oh okay, um one second."

The lock clicked open and the woman started to open the door. Before it was open more than two inches, Tommy hit it hard, forcing it open violently, and sent the woman across the room, where she landed flat on the floor. She let out a yelp from the pain of her boney ass bouncing off the hardwood. Tommy was on top of her in a flash, cupping her mouth closed with his left hand while Stein scanned the room.

In a low voice, Tommy asked, "Is he here? Is Benny here?" The woman slightly shook her head no. "Don't fucking move and don't make a sound, do you understand me?" The woman nodded.

With his gun pointed at her, Tommy stood up, put his left index finger over his mouth, reminding her to be quiet. He pointed to her in silence while making eye contact with Stein so he understood to keep an eye on her.

He made his way through the filthy apartment to the next room, which was the bedroom: Nothing but a mattress on the floor with dirty sheets and clothing strewn about. He carefully opened the closet door... nothing.

Tommy back-tracked through the living room, passed the empty bathroom and into the kitchen: nothing but trash piled about four feet high in the corner and dirty dishes in the sink.

No dining room furniture in the kitchen and no living room furniture in the living room, just scattered pieces of clothing, empty pizza boxes, a stained sheet and towel acting as curtains, empty glassine envelopes that once held heroin, and cockroaches--both dead and alive--all about the place.

"Sharon Stiles," Tommy said in a loud, commanding voice, not yelling but in the manner of a drill sergeant addressing new recruits.

"What? Yes what?" Sharon shook. Her eyes were as wide open as they could possibly be. "What! What did I do? What do you want? Oh God. Oh God are you gonna kill me? What do you want?" She babbled, her skinny body in shock, shaking.

"We want Benny and you're going to tell us where he is right fucking now, right fucking now, Sharon," Tommy demanded, leaning down eye-to-eye with her. "Tell me now," he repeated in that loud stern voice.

"Oh God oh God. I don't know, God please God I don't know. He's out but he'll be back, please don't hurt him, please don't kill me please. I don't know, I only know he'll be back."

"When?" Tommy said in a slightly less demanding tone.

"Not sure...soon. Maybe an hour, maybe more, I'm not sure! Oh God don't hurt me please...What does he owe you? How much? Is it money, is it for drugs? I got nothing to do with his shit, please know that, please don't hurt me."

Tommy smiled at Stein, who smirked slightly back, and put his weapon back into its holster. He placed a hand on both of Sharon Stiles arms, lifted her straight up, and placed her on her feet. She stared at him with her eyes wide and then he put both of her hands on top of her head. Holding them at the wrists with one hand, he quickly patted her down.

"Do you have any works in your pockets, honey, anything that may hurt me?"

She sighed and went slightly limp, almost falling to the floor.

"You're not gonna kill me, are you? You're the police... Fuck I thought you were some mafia fucks coming to kill us! Fuck fuck fuck fuck fuck...you're the police. What did he do? I know I didn't do nothing. What he do?"

"Hey, get a hold of Doreen or Jimmy," Tommy said to Stein, "Tell them to get a couple others and wait on both ends of the block. We'll wait for this kid here, and if he runs they'll be able to close in." Then he focused on Sharon Stiles again. Tommy asked, "You tell me, Sharon, what has your Benny been up to?"

"Fuck I don't know what you're asking me. Jesus. What are you doing here, am I under arrest? Do you want *me* for something?" Sharon whined.

"Don't know, Sharon. We need to talk to Benny, and we may need to talk to you also, so let's put some more clothes on and get yourself a jacket, okay?" Tommy replied.

"But am I--are you arresting me? Am I under arrest? I don't understand... Oh God what is going on? You scared me so bad, I thought you were going to hurt me. I don't know anything about anything, really I don't," Sharon pleaded.

"Relax, Sharon, we're going to go to the Precinct and ask you some questions, that's all. Come on now and get dressed. We're just going to wait for Benny before we head over... he's on his way, right?"

- 83 -

"Yes, he's on his way," she mumbled.

Minutes passed and Stein announced, "Doreen says they're on the street and have the BRAM (Burglary Robbery Apprehension Module) team on the other end of the block."

They waited for another twenty minutes, until Stein's phone beeped again. "They got him... Jimmy and Doreen grabbed him without incident as he hit the corner," Stein said with a broad smile on his face.

"Outstanding," Tommy replied, "You see, it's going to be a good night, Sharon. We found Benny and no one was hurt. C'mon now, let's take a ride and sort some stuff out."

Tommy helped her up off the floor by her bony arm and guided her to the door that Stein held open. Tommy and Stein smiled at each other as they left the roach-infested apartment.

Chapter Ten

Tommy, Stein, and Sharon arrived at the Station House, just after Doyle and Colletti. They were happy to see only one news van outside the Precinct.

Tommy smirked at Stein as they passed the petite blonde reporter cursing herself for missing Doyle, Colletti, and Hirschle's quick entry along with the chance to be the first to ask if Benny Hirschle was the murderous savage.

The trio walked up the stairs to the second floor. Stein held his hand up to stop Tommy and Sharon before he entered the squad room so he could find out where they had put Benny Hirschle.

They wanted to keep the couple separated before, during, and after their questioning.

He nodded to Colletti, "Where is he?"

"We put him in the interview room," Colletti answered.

Stein stuck his head back out the door, "Come on, bring her in," he said to Tommy.

Tommy walked Sharon Stiles to Doyle's desk and she nervously looked at the cage. "Listen Sharon," he said, more quietly this time, "I am going to take these cuffs off of you, okay? You've been really easy to deal with so far. I want to leave them off. So you're not going to misbehave, are you? You're going to sit here like a lady and answer my questions, and maybe we'll see if we can get you home sometime soon. But if you decide to fuck around and make this difficult, well I promise you, Sharon, I promise I can be much more difficult than you can be... Do you understand me? Are we in agreement?"

Sharon looked him in the eye for a moment and then lowered her eyes to the floor, "Yes, I understand. I won't be difficult. I promise."

"Okay, great. That's what I wanted to hear. Now turn around and let's get those cuffs off, then sit next to this desk right here."

Tommy sat down at the desk, then looked over to Colletti, "Hey Jimmy, do me a favor will ya and get this young lady a candy bar and a soda from the machines? What do you like, honey?" he said to Sharon.

"Uh...um, a Coke or Pepsi please... and um something with peanuts maybe? A Payday or Snickers if they have it... please," she said, her eyes never leaving the floor.

"Listen," Tommy scooted his chair in and continued in a softer low voice. He leaned in slightly to confine the space and make Sharon feel as though it were more of a personal conversation, "I don't think you are in trouble, Sharon, I don't. But I do think Benny is, and in order to help yourself and to help Benny, you're going to have to be honest with me, okay? This is one of those things that could be very serious or a complete misunderstanding, but if you lie... if you jerk me around here, it is definitely going to come back to bite you in the ass, and Benny also. So please, let's restart tonight here and now, my questions will be few and simple. Answer them honestly and maybe we can all get out of here soon, okay?"

"Ah okay. Yes okay... but what did I do? What did Benny do?" she mumbled.

"Where were you early yesterday morning, Sharon?" Tommy began.

"At home on 103rd where you came and got me."

"Where was Benny yesterday morning, Sharon?"

"Uhh... um, I don't know?"

"C'mon kid. You two live together, where was he early yesterday morning?"

"We only kinda live together... you know, it's like casual? I didn't get up till like maybe, I don't even know, one in the afternoon maybe? And he was home when I got up."

"Okay, so you wake up mid-day and Benny is there with you, yes?"

"Yes, yes that's correct. See I don't know where Benny was or coulda been because, because I was sleeping... I usually don't get up till later in the day."

"So where would Benny have gone so early in the morning, Sharon? I know you spend most of your time together. I know you know everything about him. If you know where he was, let us know. It will help you get out of here, and if it puts him in a place other than where we think he may have been, it will help him to go home as well. So, where do you think your Benny was early yesterday morning, Sharon?"

"He... he, we usually cop first thing in the morning... almost every morning," she turned her head away, a tear running down her cheek.

"Okay, so you both went to cop some junk early yesterday morning. Where did you go?"

"No," her head snapped back up and she looked at Tommy, "I didn't go with him. I sometimes go, but mostly Benny goes for both of us. It's like, how we do it. I'll hustle a few tricks and he'll cop for us both, then we'll get high and do it again the next day, you know. It's like well, like our arrangement, you know? I know he went to cop because we got high when I got up, but yeah I was home asleep till like one o'clock. That's the truth, Officer, I was asleep. Then I did nothing all day except a trick at like maybe five in the afternoon. Then I nodded off till you showed up."

"Okay, so where do you and Benny usually cop?"

Sharon lowered her head and shifted in the chair, picked at her jeans.

"We got a couple spots, but mostly above the cleaners on 93rd off First. That's the usual spot we use."

"And always in the morning?"

"Yeah, pretty much always in the morning."

"Do you know for sure if that's where Benny copped yesterday? Did he tell you that?"

"I don't think he told me that, but it's our usual spot, ya know. And it had the stamp from there, the Ernie and Bert stamp that they use over there, so yeah... Yeah, that's where he went."

"See, Sharon? It's easy to tell the truth and this may help you both in the end. You were home all day and all night and Benny went out to cop for you both yesterday morning-- that we got. Can you tell me where he was all day today?"

"Um yeah... I was home for maybe like the last three days. I didn't leave once, and Benny went out to the same place to cop some Bert and Ernie for us each morning. And one afternoon, and that's it."

"Well, where was he when we picked you up tonight?"

"He went over to the Dominicans on 97th and Lex to get some food for us. That's it. We were in the apartment the whole time except for when he went to cop or get some pizza or to Dominicans for rice and beans. Or if, if a trick came by... then he would go downstairs and wait till they left...that's it, we were together every other time."

"Okay. Good. Remember when he got locked up for fighting with the priest awhile back?"

"Yes," Sharon said lowering her eyes to the floor once again.

"Okay, what can you tell me about that?"

"Um, nothing really. We would steal shit from churches sometimes and then sell whatever we got...bibles and shit. Sometimes we could get into the donation box. Then one day that priest caught us. Benny pushed him back so's we could run but the priest got ahold of him and beat him up and called the cops and then you guys charged him with some other shit from other churches."

"Well, did you steal from the other churches?"

"Well yeah, probably, but I don't really know which ones. So maybe."

"Does Benny hate the church or hate priests, do you think?"

"No, Benny could care less... he knew he was wrong. We know we're wrong man. Look at us... Fuck, we can't get mad. People hate us for what we do, we get that… you think we want to live like this?"

"No, I know you don't, Sharon. Believe me, I know you don't, kid."

Colletti walked back into the squad room with a Coke and a Payday candy bar and walked over to where Tommy and Sharon sat.

"Hey Jimmy, sit with her a minute while I talk to Stein, will ya?" Tommy stepped away from the desk and moved behind Sharon, gesturing to Jimmy to be quiet and not ask her any questions.

"Sure thing," Colletti replied.

Chapter Eleven

Tommy and Stein converged in the hallway outside of the squad room next to the PAA's desk. Stein pushed his glasses up and looked inside the room at the back of Sharon Stiles, ripping open the candy bar. He turned back to face Tommy.

"So what did she give you, Tom?" asked Stein.

"She puts him in the direction of the school, says they cop heroin on 93rd off First, so depending on which way he walks, he could go right past the school. She doesn't seem to know anything about what we are looking at him for, and I'd like to keep it that way until we charge him anyway. She's been very cooperative and my guess is she's clueless."

"Okay, you want to sit in the Box with me? Or watch it through the window?" asked Stein.

"Which do you prefer?" asked Keane.

"Either works for me."

"I'll watch. I'll see if I can put anything together, then maybe join you."

"Okay, good. Let's do it then."

Tommy nodded, walked down the hall and entered the observation room while Stein entered the interrogation room.

***

"Hello, Benjamin, I'm Detective Stein. Do you remember me?" Stein said as he walked into the room and closed the door behind him. The interview room, or the Box as they sometimes called it, was a tiny room. There was one desk with a chair on each side. The room was soundproof with a bench placed along the wall to one side, a two way mirror at the back, and a camera in the corner that recorded the interviews.

"Yes," was Benny's one word answer.

"Can you tell me why the other detectives picked you up tonight?" Stein asked as he pulled out the metal chair from the table and sat across from Benjamin Hirschle.

"Yeah, I had some junk on me. I heard some shit about a nun on the way in but, I didn't rob no nun. I don't know anything bout any nun or any robbery," Benny said, scratching at his face with dirty fingernails.

"Can you tell me where you were early yesterday morning, Benny?"

"Yeah. I was at home. All day all night. Just me and my girl," Benny grinned at Stein.

"Really, all day and all night. You sure about that?" Stein asked.

"Sure as shit, man. All day and all night, at home with my girl. You want you can go ask her. She lives over by where those other cops grabbed me," Benny said sitting back in his chair, smiling.

"Okay, we may just do that. So again... yesterday morning... this is what I am asking, where were you yesterday morning?"

"At home, in my apartment on 103rd, same block as those cops grabbed me at not like maybe an hour ago."

"Okay, so no matter how many times I ask you, that's your answer right? Home with your girl all day and all night?"

"Right, you got it."

"Now, I'll ask you again. And this time I'll let you know we have you on camera, walking toward 93rd Street yesterday morning, and it looks like you are wearing pretty much the same clothes you are wearing today. Now Benny does that jar your memory at all? Can you tell me where you were yesterday morning?"

"How do you know it's me on the camera?" Benny asked sitting up straight, slightly angered, scratching his scalp, "Could be a thousand guys heading out for work, or something, passing those cameras every morning."

Stein sat back in the chair shaking his head, "No, it's not a thousand other guys, Benny. It's you. Now how bout you cut the shit and tell me where you were yesterday morning."

Benny cackled, "Or what, you gonna rough me up? You gonna get physical with me like that one who picked me up? Man I ain't scared. I didn't do nothin. I didn't rob no one. I been, I been living okay since I got outta Rikers and you ain't got nothing on me, man, nothing but a little bit of heroin I just bought today."

"Let me ask you Benny. You mad at me for locking you up for those church burglaries?"

"No. I know it's your job."

"You mad at the priest for catching you breaking into the poor box at the church?"

"No, not really. Well, he didn't have to fuck me up. I mean, he's a priest. He could've shown some patience you know, that wasn't cool him kicking my ass." Benny rubbed his face vigorously with his scabbed hands.

"Didn't you fight back when he grabbed you?"

"Hell no... I would never hit a Father, a man of the cloth, no way," Benny sat up straight again, "I wasn't raised that way. I tried to run. I did. I mighta pushed him back when he tried to grab my girl, but no way, no way did I try to fight him. No way. Fuck, he just yoked me, you know, and beat me down to the floor. Unnecessary, totally unnecessary, the way he beat me."

"And you're not angry?" Stein asked sitting back in his chair.

"Okay, yeah, maybe a little angry. I think it was wrong to beat me down like that. Fuck it was a couple of bibles and a couple a bucks that's all, we didn't hurt no one."

"Would you have liked to hurt him, Benny? Maybe get back at the church?"

"What? With like some lawsuit shit?" Benny cackled, "Yeah I can see that, some low life like me suing the Catholic Church for getting punched around after stealing some money and some bibles. Yeah that would happen! How many churches you charge me with, Detective? Six right? Yeah no, I think no lawyer in the country would take that case."

"Would you like to kick that priest's ass, Benny? You know, to make things even?"

"Nope. No. Like I said, I wasn't brought up that way."

"So you're a religious guy? Believe in the church, is that it?"

"No, I got nothing to do with the church, but I respect it. I don't practice or nothin but I know it's important to a lot of people. Just not to me is all."

"So you don't hate it. Are you angry with the church for putting you in Rikers, Benny?"

"Listen," Benny raised his voice and slapped his hand on the table, "I don't know what you are getting at. I think the church coulda shown a little compassion for me, yeah--that's what they're supposed to be about, right? And I don't think that Father over at Saint Dominic's shoulda beaten me like that. That's really wrong! Kindness is supposed to be his thing right? But I'm telling you outright, I didn't rob no nun and I was in my house all day and all night yesterday. Boom! Case closed." Benny slammed his palm on the table top again and sat back in the metal chair, smirking at Stein.

Tommy knocked lightly on the scarred interrogation room door. Stein replied from behind the door, "Yeah come in."

Tommy entered the room and closed the door behind him. He stood by the side of the table with his hands in his pockets.

"Benny, this is Detective Keane. He's going to join us for a bit." Benny looked up at Tommy with a smirk and raised his palms up in surrender.

"Whoa. Is this where one of you gets rough with me? Like good cop bad cop shit?"

"Benny, stop. We don't do that kind of stuff. We just need to ask you some questions, okay? And we need some honest answers," Tommy said calmly, sitting down on the wooden bench and leaning forward with his forearms on his thighs.

"Yeah, uh okay. I been honest with you so far. Go ahead."

Tommy continued, speaking softer, so Benny leaned towards him. "Well, this is what we know: We know you were in the vicinity of Our Lady of Perpetual Hope on 93rd Street yesterday morning. We know this because we have you on camera walking there and then leaving there. We also have information from your girl Sharon that you and her regularly cop at the spot on 93rd and First. We also know that there are numerous glassine envelopes with the Bert and Ernie stamp all over your apartment on 103rd Street--the stamp that comes from the spot on 93rd off First. This we know. This is fact, this is the truth and we have it, we physically have it. We also have the four glassine envelopes stamped with Bert and Ernie that you had on your person when the detectives grabbed you tonight. Now... what we would like to know is why on your way to cop on 93rd and First, like you do almost every morning, did you stop by Our Lady of Perpetual Hope?"

"Oh. Okay so you spoke to Sharon? When did she tell you all of this?"

"Yes, we spoke to Sharon, Benny. I had a long conversation with her and she told me all about how you two cop over at Bert and Ernie's almost daily. She also told me how much you hate the Catholic Church and how much you hate that priest who had you arrested... and how you pimp her out over there on 103rd Street just so you can afford your habit."

"Whoa, what! Hold on!" Benny jerked back away from Tommy, "I don't pimp her out at all. She's my girl and I love her. She does what she does on her own. To support us! We look out for each other! I would never hurt her and if it was up to me she wouldn't do any of that shit. Yes. Yes, I copped at that spot yesterday. So what? We're fiends. That's what we do. And fuck that Father Dominic, he's a fucking bully! Fuck, look at the size of me and that priest is built like the Hulk. How was I gonna hurt him? We was trying to run is all, just trying to run."

Benny began to cry in anger. "Fuck that priest," he shouted, "and fuck the church and fuck all of you! Okay? Fuck all of you. You don't know how hard it is for us..." He was quiet for a moment, then, "So yeah, I was there. I walked past that school--I do almost every morning. But I didn't rob no nun. I didn't do nothing but get some fucking dope and go home. That's it!"

"Alright Benny, relax," said Stein. "Now we are getting somewhere."

"Hey Benny, can I get you a soda or something?" asked Tommy.

"Fuck you guys," Benny replied.

***

Tommy and Stein stepped outside the interrogation room and headed to Lieutenant Bricks' office. Stein knocked on the closed door, waited, then opened it at Bricks' command. He and Tommy entered the small room and shut the door behind them while Bricks glanced up from his paperwork, an expectant look on his face.

Stein started, "Well Lu, it's no confession, but we have him, and her putting him at the scene. We have the video footage of him going to and coming from the scene. We have nothing back from any forensics yet, but it's a good chance this might be our guy. Let's get Crime Scene over to their apartment and see what they come up with. We'll print him, charge him for the heroin he had on him tonight and hold her for a while as well, see if we can charge her with anything we find in the apartment. We got some hours to go but hopefully by tomorrow we'll have what we need."

Bricks smiled at the detectives. "Okay, great work men. I'll call the DA's office and let them and the Captain know. I'm glad you wrapped this one up quickly, I hate to think of that animal out on the streets still." He shook his head, and said, "Finish up what you have to tonight and go get some sleep."

Tommy and Stein nodded and left the office, shutting the door behind them. Before entering the main squad room, Tommy leaned toward Stein and quietly spoke, "You wanna come talk to Sharon now, see if we can get a little more out of her?"

"Yeah, let's see what else she can give us."

Tommy and Stein headed toward Doyle's desk where Sharon sat slumped over in the chair, her eyes barely open. Her can of Coke was tucked between her bony legs.

"Jimmy, give me your seat please?" Stein asked. Jimmy jumped up and Stein dragged the chair over to Doyle's desk. He sat directly in front of Sharon and spoke quietly, "Sharon, I'm Detective Stein. You remember me from your apartment a few hours ago?" She looked at him without lifting her head, staring up with only her eyes.

"Uh yeah," she mumbled.

"Just a few questions for you, Sharon. I know you already spoke to Detective Keane here, but I'd just like to see if I can get you to help me understand a little more," Stein continued.

"Okay. Uh yeah... go ahead," she replied.

"Great thanks... I want to ask you about Benny and the priest. It was me who arrested him for that robbery, did you know that?"

"I wasn't sure," she replied. "You know that priest beat him up pretty bad that night, you ever think about arresting him?"

"No, we're not in the habit of arresting robbery victims who defend themselves and their property, Sharon. Can you tell me if Benny held a grudge against the priest who beat him?"

She shook her head, "No, he didn't."

"None whatsoever?" asked Stein as he raised his eyebrows at her. "He got banged up pretty bad that night, took a couple of stitches, too... Did he never once say he wanted to get back at that priest or the church, Sharon? Never?"

Sharon took a deep breath and sat up in her chair a little, "Yeah, he was pissed off when I went to visit him at Rikers, I guess. Saying shit about wantin to burn the church down with that priest in it... but that was just angry talk cause he was so pissed about getting beat and locked up is all."

"Do you think he could have, or would have, ever acted on those feelings, Sharon? You know, could he have really burned a church or killed a priest? Do you think he has the balls to do something like that?"

Sharon snapped her head up and looked incensed. "My Benny has plenty of balls, man... Do you think cause he's small he ain't tough? Benny is very tough; you have to be to live like we do."

"I believe it," Stein replied, nodding his head, "So you think he's tough enough to kill someone?"

"Sure he is," Sharon said almost defiantly, as if she were being challenged. "Benny can handle himself, yeah! He's protected me a few times from guys much bigger than he is-- stood right up to them and didn't back down. Benny can be real tough when he needs to be."

"Okay... I thought he was tougher than he looked, sure. What happened when he fought the priest, Sharon? It sounds like you were there?"

Sharon lowered her gaze from Stein and dropped her shoulders a bit. "Well... well, we got caught stealing and Benny stood up to the priest so I could run... that's all I really saw. I ran and the priest beat him up and you guys arrested him. That's all I know."

"And then he said he would burn the church with the priest in it."

"Yeah... but he was just pissed. You know, just pissed at the situation."

"Okay, Sharon, I'm going to show you some pictures now. Just take a second. This is from yesterday morning on 93rd Street. It's a still of Benny. You see we know that he was going to cop for you two on 93rd." Stein placed a photo from the surveillance camera on the desk so Sharon could see it. "This is another one of Benny from another camera. You do agree this is Benny, yes?"

"Um uh yeah. Yes that looks like Benny," she replied.

"You're sure or you think?" Stein asked.

"Yeah, that's him."

"Who?"

"Benny," she replied.

"Okay. Now take a good look at this photo and tell me if you recognize this person at all." Stein placed a photo of Sister Margaret's mutilated body on the desk. "Is Benny tough enough to do this, Sharon?"

Sharon's eyes opened wide. Her breathing paused for a few seconds as her brain processed the image, and then she let out a blood curdling shriek that made everyone in the office jump.

"Noooo. Benny, no...What did you do? Oh my god, Benny, what did you do?" Her voice got higher and more panicked as she rocked back and forth in her chair. "God damn it, Benny, god damn it no!" Then she stopped shrieking and began to sob and shake uncontrollably.

Stein put his hand on her shoulder. "It's okay, Sharon. Breathe, Sharon, it's okay," Stein said in a soft, soothing voice.

Lieutenant Bricks, who had come out of his office and was standing next to Keane, said in a muffled tone, "Looks like we got our man."

Sister Margaret

Chapter Twelve

Tommy woke abruptly to the alarm. He reached over and shut it off with a sigh. He had managed to get about three hours of sleep after completing his twenty-hour shift, and he rolled out of bed and forced out his fifty pushups, feeling broken from head to toe.

He showered and dressed and headed out the apartment door as quickly as he could, leaving quietly so as not to disturb his mother, who was still in bed.

He stepped out onto the stoop, scanning the block from left to right. It was a cold and wet October morning, and he wasn't feeling the walk he so usually enjoyed, so he grabbed a cab on Second Avenue and rode to work.

Once again, Tommy was the first of the squad to arrive in the office. He took off his leather coat and sat in Doyle's chair. He swiveled it to the right so he could look out the dirty window at the cold rain that was still falling, and sat quietly as the rest of the squad rolled in, exchanging good mornings and pleasantries with one another as the day began.

Once Sergeant Browne arrived and made himself comfortable, he called out, "Stein, Keane, come in here please."

Tommy got up from the chair and followed Stein into the room. "Good job last night and this week with this nun homicide, really good job. I assume you still have follow up work to do on this case, so I'd like the two of you to do whatever it is you need to do to tie this all up. I'll have Doyle and Colletti get back to their cases. There is supposed to be a press meeting with the Captain about this one at 2pm. Please be back well before then, he's going to want to talk to you and the press may also."

"A press meeting?" Stein replied, "We haven't charged anyone with this homicide yet. How can there be a press meeting about it?"

Tommy shook his head in disbelief, agreeing with Stein.

"I have no idea what's going on," Sergeant Browne added, "I only know what's on this sheet of paper in front of me, and it says 'Stein and Keane press conference 2pm.'"

"Okay...well I guess we have a conference then," Stein replied.

Both Stein and Keane stepped out from Sergeant Browne's office.

"What the fuck is going on?" Tommy whispered to Stein.

"This is going to be a Peleggi thing, I guarantee it," Stein said, "We haven't even charged the kid yet and he's calling in the press to get his face on the evening news. This man is unbelievable."

"I'd like to head back to the school and go over the crime scene again, especially if we have to be back by two," Tommy said to Stein.

"Exactly what I was thinking," Stein replied as he grabbed his coat from the back of his chair, "We won't have anything back from the lab for a while so I think it's the best place to start today."

***

Stein and Keane arrived at the school and were greeted by Sister Claire, a tall, thin woman with haunting dark brown eyes.

"Bless you. Bless you boys for catching that awful man who did this to our good Sister Margaret," she said, shaking their hands and bowing her head to each. "And God bless the NYPD for all of God's work you do each day."

"Thank you very much, Sister," Both men replied simultaneously.

They followed Sister Claire down the hallway to Sister Margaret's office. Sister Claire unlocked the door in solemn silence, and then left the two detectives alone. Tommy pulled a small stag-handled push-button switchblade from his pocket, and snapped it open to cut through the Crime Scene sticker that sealed the door and the jamb.

"Hey, switchblades are illegal in New York," Stein said.

Tommy turned and winked at him. "So call a cop," he replied as they opened the room and both stood in the doorway. Stein switched on the light and the detectives slowly stepped inside, taking in everything that was around them.

The room hadn't been touched since they last left it-- the only visible difference was the fingerprint residue left by the Evidence Collection Unit, which covered most of the room. Tommy once again stood in front of Sister Margaret's grey metal desk and looked up at the large four-foot crucifix that hung on the wall behind her chair. Looking into Jesus' mournful eyes he mumbled, "If only you could talk, pal."

Keane and Stein searched silently through everything in the office. Slowly and methodically, they combed through the closet, the desk drawers, and the two bookcases. The room was fairly small, with no windows, and was impeccably tidy, something Stein made mention of.

"I can't believe how neat this room is."

"What's that they say about cleanliness being next to godliness?" Tommy replied.

"And look at all these awards and accolades on the walls. There are photos of her with the last three mayors, and here's one with a governor... Seems Sister Margaret was pretty well-liked in this city," Stein remarked.

"Yeah looks like she had some strong political and business ties," Tommy replied, thoughtfully.

After a solid ninety minutes of searching and leafing through papers, books, and files, Stein asked Tommy, "Anything, Tommy? Do you see anything that might help nail this guy?"

"No," Tommy replied, "Nothing here that seems like evidence to me. Hopefully Crime Scene has something. I have to say I have never seen a cleaner--or should I say less-disturbed--crime scene. I see no evidence of any struggle or fight, nothing out of place. Just these few scuff marks here on the floor in front of her chair. But even they seem kind of...subtle, if that makes sense. They look a little out of place, but not violent. Did you notice them?"

"Yes, I assumed they're from her shoes pushing the chair in and out from under her desk," Stein replied. "It looks that way to me, and I have to agree, they don't look like they were caused violently. I'm curious to read the ME's final report."

They left the office and had Sister Claire lock the door, which Stein resealed with a new NYPD sticker. Then, they headed over to Benny and Sharon's apartment on 103rd Street, where again they cut through the crime scene seal once the super unlocked the door, and searched diligently for the next hour.

While the apartment was much larger and much, much dirtier than Sister Margaret's tidy little office, it was every bit as easy to search simply because Benny and Sharon owned nothing. Both Stein and Keane quickly went through the few belongings the couple had. They started with the small pile of dirty clothes on the floor of the closet, searching through each pocket of every garment, and came up with twelve cents and a couple of empty glassine envelopes, stamped Bert and Ernie.

The couple had no furniture, with the exception of a filthy mattress and one pillow on the bedroom floor and two folding beach chairs in the living area, one of which was missing part of the seat. There was a radio sitting on top of the refrigerator, which was almost empty except for a slice of pizza, a half empty container of Lo Mein, and two cans of Pepsi.

The bathroom had two stained towels hanging on a hook on the door, two rolls of toilet paper on the back of the toilet, and a small trash can with three empty douche applicators and some used condoms. The detectives found more empty glassine envelopes and a small zippered cosmetics bag under the mattress which contained some lipstick, a drugstore brand eyeliner, and heroin works.

Stein and Keane looked everywhere and at everything but really there was nothing for them to search. Like most junkies, Benny and Sharon would sell anything of value, and the only incriminating evidence in the apartment was of their drug use and prostitution, neither of which currently concerned the detectives.

***

Disappointed after two fruitless searches, Tommy and Stein returned to the Station House where they met with Lieutenant Bricks.

"So what did you fellas dig up?" Bricks asked.

Stein shook his head, "Not a thing, Lu. The Sister's office gave us nothing and the kids' apartment... well, there was nothing in it for it to give. The place was filthy but pretty much barren, no sign of any link to this homicide that we could see."

"Alright, hopefully Crime Scene will deliver something solid," Lieutenant Bricks replied. "Hey, get downstairs and brief the captain and don't disappear. There's going to be a press thing at two."

"Yes sir. Sergeant Browne informed us. So this press briefing is for--" Stein replied but was cut off by Lieutenant Bricks.

"It's for bullshit. It's our illustrious Captain leaking some nothing-information to the press to try and capitalize on your work and on a perp who hasn't even been charged yet. The man is an idiot, what can I say? Just be sure you're back by two."

"Yes sir, we'll be there."

Both Keane and Stein walked down the stairs to the first floor and told the desk sergeant on duty they needed to see the captain. The sergeant--a fat, balding man with a red face--

nodded to them and said, "Good fucking job guys" with a wink and a thumbs up, before announcing them to the captain.

Captain Peleggi gestured them into his cramped office and immediately told them to sit down as he congratulated them on their swift arrest of Benjamin Hirschle.

"Good work, Detectives," Captain Peleggi exclaimed, "This was an unbelievably grizzly murder and you men were able to find and catch the killer in less than forty-eight hours. Excellent work, thank you. We have a press conference in a couple of hours and I would like you to share the details of the case with me so I can inform the press accurately of the work we've done here this week."

'The work we've done here this week?' Tommy thought to himself. He knew where this was going. Neither Tommy nor Stein had any desire to talk to the press about this case--even though a suspect had been arrested there was a lot of work to do before they could charge Benny Hirschle for Sister Margaret's murder.

Tommy knew Captain Peleggi had to answer to headquarters, and to the media. This was a "big press case" and he understood that, but 'the work *we've* done here this week?' This man was going to insert himself into this investigation and put his own name and face on the arrest.

'Just like an empty suit,' Tommy thought, 'he's trying to soak up the limelight for the murder of this poor woman. Fucking opportunist.'

Captain Peleggi asked the men a few basic questions about the case and about Benny's apprehension, and Stein answered patiently. Finally, he said, "But Captain...we haven't charged Hirschle with this crime yet. I know you know that, but I really think--"

"I don't care what you think, Detective. Your evidence is circumstantial but it's strong. I'm certain you have the right man, and as soon as the lab comes back with some blood or prints putting Hirschle in that room, it will most definitely be 'Case Closed.' Very good then."

Captain Peleggi stood and hitched at his pants, "I'll see you men in the Muster Room at 1:45."

The detectives left the office and closed the door behind them. They stood by the front door of the precinct, and Stein asked, "Hungry?"

"Eh, not really, but I could eat," Tommy replied and they stepped outside.

Chapter Thirteen

When they arrived back at the precinct just before 1:30, the place was already abuzz with press. Tommy and Stein headed straight up to the Muster Room, an open and airy space with large arched windows facing the street. There was a podium set up at the far end of the room and the chairs facing it were full of anxious-looking reporters.

Tommy, Stein, Lieutenant Bricks, and Sergeant Browne were all directed to stand behind the podium. Captain Peleggi stood at the podium, center stage, and thanked the press for coming. The show began.

"I'd very much like to thank the press for coming today. I know you have been waiting to speak with us directly about the horrific homicide of the beloved Sister Margaret, but please understand that while we were investigating this crime, we had to keep most of the known details of the case to ourselves until an arrest was made. I'm happy to report that the 21st Detective Squad, under my direct supervision, has made that arrest and has taken one Benjamin Hirschle off the streets. No doubt protecting more innocent victims from this violent and disturbing individual."

"Yes?" He prompted, pointing to a raised hand in the group of journalists and photographers assembled before him.

"Do you know if he intended to kill more clergy?" the reporter asked.

"We can't speculate on that, but we do know that he attacked a Catholic priest once before in the past," Captain Peleggi replied, and continued, "Yes?" He pointed to another reporter.

"Is he a Satanist, or a member of ISIS?" the reporter asked.

"As of this moment we do not know what his religious leanings are, or if he is a member of any terrorist group. What we can say is that he has been arrested for the brutal murder of this nun and has previously been arrested and convicted of attacking a priest."

"Yes?" to another reporter.

"So it is possible this man belongs to a Satanist group or a terrorist cell?" The reporter asked.

"We can't confirm or deny either of those possibilities."

"But they are possibilities?"

"We are looking into those and every other possibility. We are investigating whether Hirschle worked alone or as part of an organized group, but at this time we have no evidence pointing us in either direction."

The questions and answers went on for another twenty minutes. When it was all over, Captain Peleggi thanked the press, posed for a few photos and left the room. Tommy couldn't stay quiet any longer; he swung around to the others.

"Are you kidding me? Can you believe how they forced things into the story that weren't there! Their questions had no basis in any sort of reality at all, and Captain Peleggi couldn't help himself could he?" Tommy went on, growing angrier. "We just sat with him two hours ago and told him the whole story. Satanist? Terrorists? ISIS? Are you fucking kidding me! We're looking into whether he worked alone or with others? No we're not, why is he saying this shit?"

"Quiet down," Lieutenant Bricks hushed him. "Believe me, this is nothing new. This man loves to showboat and he loves the attention. It's got nothing to do with the case and we know that, and those fuckers are going to print whatever they want in their rags anyway. Fuck 'em. You guys got the guy and that's all that matters."

"Listen, Tom," Stein added, "This is a big deal for the press and, politically, it's a big deal for the Captain. He's gonna milk it for as much attention as he can get. We took care of things on our end, so forget about his self-important promotion-seeking bullshit. We got Sister Margaret's killer. Let's tie up all the loose ends on this case, take a break for the next couple of days, and get ready for whatever the city throws at us next week," Stein continued. "Like the Lu said, this is business as usual."

The three headed back down to the squad room and recounted the experience to Doyle and Colletti. Then each staff member signed out for the evening and for the following two days. Finally, they could rest--they had closed a case by arrest, one of the most heinous crimes to have been committed in the 2-1 in recent history.

Sister Margaret

Chapter Fourteen

Tommy started down the steps, putting on his leather car coat and buttoning it up to brace himself against the cold. He passed the captain talking to two reporters who were undoubtedly asking him questions about the Sister Margaret case.

Captain Peleggi's and Tommy's eyes met momentarily as Tommy passed him, and the captain quickly looked away, focusing back on the reporters.

'Yup. He knows he's a cunt,' Tommy thought to himself.

He stepped out into the cold dark October evening and began to walk home. The rain had subsided and although there was a bite to the bitter air, Tommy felt he could use a good walk to decompress a bit. As he approached the corner he saw the young reporter from the diner leaning up against a car.

"Detective? Detective Keane," the young reporter called as he pushed himself off the car, "May I ask you a few questions, sir? I'm--"

Tommy cut him off, "I remember you. Gil from the diner. You're the kid that interrupted my sandwich but then was kind enough to pay for it."

"Yes sir, that's me. Gil Nunez," Gil stuck out his hand to shake, but Tommy's hands never left his pockets. Gil went on, "I'd like to--"

Tommy interrupted him again, "No. I don't talk to reporters."

"Please, Detective, I'd like to tell the real story of Sister Margaret's murder."

"The answer is no," Tommy brushed passed him and continued walking, "I don't talk to reporters."

"Thank you, Detective. Have a good night, and thanks for catching that bastard."

Tommy stopped at the curb and waited for the walk light to appear. When it did he stepped off the curb and then stopped short and turned around. Nunez was already walking back towards the precinct.

"Hey kid! Nunez," Tommy shouted down the street. Gil Nunez turned back towards Tommy. Tommy motioned him back, "Come on. Come take a walk with me and I'll answer some questions."

Gil's face broke into a broad, triumphant smile, and he ran to meet Tommy on the corner.

"Listen kid, I'll answer your questions and I'll fill you in a little on this story, but you're not gonna print anything I don't say or twist anything I tell you into some bullshit that didn't happen to try and sell your fucking papers. You understand me? I don't want to come find you tomorrow morning and have to tune you up because you put some shit in the paper that never happened. You're also not going to mention my name or cite any sources, you got that?"

Gil was still grinning like a kid on Christmas morning, "I got it! Tune me up?"

"Yeah, tune you up. You know... give you a beating," Tommy replied.

"Oh. No sir," Gil responded, shaking his head, "I want to tell this story properly. I want your insights and as many facts as you can share, and I promise it will all be completely confidential."

"Alright. Come walk with me," Tommy replied and stepped off the curb to cross the avenue.

They walked east until they got to First Avenue and then headed north. On the way, Tommy answered Gil's questions and elaborated on details whenever he felt it was necessary. He also let Gil know in no uncertain terms that Captain Peleggi had no reason to call a news conference for a case which was still open, and that Benny Hirschle was currently only being held on drug possession charges. By the time the two reached 85th Street, Tommy felt the young reporter should have enough information on the case to write it out in its entirety.

"You good?" Tommy asked standing on the southwest corner of 85th Street and First Avenue, "You got all you need?"

"Yes I, I think so," Gil replied. "Thank you. Thank you so much, Detective. You don't know how much I appreciate and respect you giving me the whole story. And so many details! I do so appreciate it."

"Very good," Tommy replied, "Now do a good job and don't make me come by wherever it is you live over some hatchet job."

"No sir, Detective. Never."

"Cool. Now you go that way," Tommy pointed west down 85th Street, "cause I'm going this way." He pointed east up 85th Street. "And enjoy the rest of your weekend."

Gil looked a little perplexed at Tommy's directions but said okay and began walking west on 85th Street while Tommy headed east towards York Avenue.

***

Once he reached the corner of 85th and York, Tommy stepped into Bailey's Corner Pub. There was a good number of people there and the place was still full of the after-work crowd. Tommy was unable to find an empty seat at the bar as he walked from one end to the other. Jack, the barman, noticed him and shouted over the din, "Tommy!" He handed Tommy a bottle of Budweiser and a shot of Jameson in a rocks glass.

Tommy stood alone at the rail that separated the bar from the rest of the room. He drank his beer and observed the crowd. Then he pulled his cell phone from his pocket and called his mother.

"Hey Ma, how you doing? Did you eat yet?…No? Can I take you out for some dinner tonight?…Okay great, Ma. I'll be home in like ten minutes to pick you up…Okay Ma, Yes, Ma…I love you too, Ma." He disconnected and put his phone back in his pocket.

'Holy fuck,' he thought to himself, 'How many Ma's was that? I'm starting to sound like the old bird myself now.' He threw down the rest of the whiskey and finished the bottle of Bud. Then he handed Jack a twenty dollar bill over the bar, said goodnight, and walked outside, heading north on York Avenue, back to his mother's apartment on 88th Street.

***

Tommy quickly changed into something fresh and more comfortable and joined his mother in the living room. He noticed she had applied a little rouge and lipstick and he smiled to himself.

"Where would you like to go, Ma?" Tommy asked.

"Oh jeez, Tommy, I don't know, Tommy. Anywhere you'd like to go Tommy is okay with me dear."

"How about the Heidelberg, Ma? We haven't been there in years."

"Oh no Tommy, that's too expensive, Tommy. Save your money. That's too expensive a place for me, Tommy."

"Nonsense Ma, you're my favorite girl and no place is too expensive for you. I know you used to love going there so let's take a walk over and have a nice meal, okay?"

"Oh Tommy... I don't know, Tommy."

"Enough Ma, come on. Let's go have a nice meal just me and you."

She stood up and smoothed out her skirt, smiling up at him.

"Tommy. It's you and I, Tommy, not me and you."

Tommy and his mother walked arm in arm down to the Heidelberg restaurant on 2nd Avenue just south of 86th Street, his mother talking the whole way like an excited school girl on her first date. She shared memories of growing up in the neighborhood, recalling details about herself, Tommy, his younger sister Kathleen, and their school years in Yorkville like they were yesterday.

They stopped at the red light at 86th Street and Tommy's mother looked up at him, concerned.

"You know I wish I could have sent you to Catholic School instead of that filthy Julia Richmond, Tommy, but I couldn't afford it Tommy. I sent your sister because she was a girl, Tommy, and she couldn't go to a public high school, Tommy, you understand, Tommy, don't you? That school wasn't fit for a young girl to go to, but I knew you were tough enough, Tommy. You've always been a tough boy, Tommy. You understand don't you, Tommy?"

"Of course I do, Ma," he hushed her and changed the subject as they made their way across the street.

They walked into the Heidelberg and paused for a moment to let their eyes adjust to the dimness. The bar to the left was full of people, all over the age of forty, having a drink with strangers before they went home to their lonely apartments. The restaurant side was nearly empty and Tommy escorted his mother to a table below the framed needlepoint of a raven-haired woman. The piece of art had been there for decades, but looking at it this time, Tommy saw the faint resemblance to his ex-wife Cookie.

They ordered drinks and a large soft homemade pretzel as an appetizer. Mrs. Keane ordered the schnitzel and Tommy ordered the goulash. They enjoyed their food slowly and talked more about the old neighborhood and the changes that were taking place there.

After their meal, they walked home again, arm in arm, Tommy's mother prattling on with old stories, all of which he had heard a thousand times. He knew she loved to reminisce, so he let her go on and on. As she talked he became certain that his mother couldn't have the beginnings of Alzheimer's Disease.

Not only did she remember every detail of their lives, she managed to get along fine with every detail of her current life. Yes, something was increasingly odd about his mother, but she was as sharp as a tack. She scheduled all of her own doctor's appointments, made it to and from the store to do the shopping, never forgot birthdays or anniversaries or anyone's name, and certainly knew the business of everyone in the building and up and down the block.

'No,' he thought, 'This sweet old girl doesn't have Alzheimer's, she's too sharp for that. I'll have to take her to another doctor and see what they think.'

Once they returned home, they sat in the living room and watched television for several hours while she talked and talked and eventually began to nod off. Tommy got her up and put her to bed, then retired himself. He turned the alarm off on his phone, hoping he would be able to sleep in a little late; both his body and his mind needed the rest.

Sister Margaret

Chapter Fifteen

Tommy's eyes opened to the complete darkness of his bedroom. He reached for his phone and was happy to see it read 9:53 am. It wasn't too early and he had gotten a full night's sleep for the first time in a long while. He tossed the quilt off of him and rolled out of bed to do his morning fifty. Then he snapped on the lamp and dressed in some grey sweatpants, a zip up hoodie, and his running shoes.

He stepped out of his room and into the kitchen, noticing his mother was already up and watching "Sunday Morning" on television. She had a half-finished quilt on her lap and a lit cigarette in the ashtray next to her.

"Good morning, Tommy. Tommy have you seen 'Sunday Morning' lately? I like Jane Pauley, Tommy, I think she is a fine woman but I so miss Charles Osgood, Tommy. I don't think the show is the same without him. You know what I miss the most, Tommy? I miss his poems and oh! when he played the piano. Do you remember, Tommy? I just loved that, Tommy."

"I know Ma, I miss Osgood too."

"What do you have planned for the day, Tommy? Oh and thank you for dinner last night, Tommy. I love the

Heidelberg. It's been years since I've been there, thank you, Tommy."

"Of course, Ma. I had a good time with you, too. I think I am gonna go for a quick run, Ma. When I get home I'll call Caitlyn and Cookie to see how everything is going."

"Give them my love, Tommy."

"Will do, Ma."

Tommy headed over to FDR Drive and ran down to the Queensboro Bridge and back. Then he sat on a bench overlooking the East River. He pulled out his cell phone and called his ex-wife. When no one answered, he left a message "Hey Cook, how you doing? Just checking in to make sure all is cool in your world, hit me back when convenient... love you."

He didn't mention anything about his week or about Sister Margaret. Tommy almost never discussed police work with his wife or family, really never with anyone outside of the cases. He hated braggers and self-promoting storytellers.

Tommy didn't need to be liked or appreciated for doing his job. His mother had always said, "Talkers aren't doers, Tommy," and it was something he took to heart. Over the years he learned that more often than not her words rang true.

He, therefore, made it a point to be closed-mouthed about a lot of things, a habit that certainly helped to strain his relationship with his now ex-wife.

Catharine "Cookie" Buonomo fell in love with and married a cop. She wasn't a cop hag by any means, but did love the look of Tommy in his uniform. She was very much attracted to the hyper-masculine image of her husband righting all the wrongs of the world in the embattled borough of the Bronx.

But the amount of time she spent alone, especially the nights alone, and the constant fear of something awful happening to him at the hands of some miscreant played on her nerves terribly.

It was soon after Tommy's longtime partner, Henry Sanchez, had his eye shot out during a buy-and-bust operation (after which Tommy took a bullet in the shoulder before killing the two perpetrators, alone on a rooftop in the Kingsbridge section of the Bronx) that their marriage began to fall apart. Cookie had a small nervous breakdown and could no longer bear to be alone at home with their then six year old daughter. She would stay awake for hours waiting for Tommy to come home. It affected her health, her job, her relationships with family members and friends and, worst of all, it affected her as a mother.

Almost a year to the date of Henry Sanchez's shooting, Tommy and Cookie were in divorce proceedings. The process was smooth and amicable. Cookie simply couldn't do it anymore, and Tommy couldn't ask her to; he loved her too much.

After leaving a message with Cookie, Tommy called his daughter, Caitlyn, who was at school at Siena College.

"Hi Daddy," she answered.

"Hey kid, how you doing?"

"I'm doing good! Bio is soooo hard, but I really love it here, my other classes aren't too tough, and I'm getting along great with my roommate, but I can't talk right now, Daddy! We're heading out to Fall Fest in Albany! I love you and I'll call you later, okay?"

"Okay sweet girl, I love you. And hey, don't do anything stupid, okay?"

"I know, and I won't."

Tommy always ended his conversations with his daughter the same way, "Don't do anything stupid." It was a simple, all-encompassing way of saying "take care of yourself" and "be smart" and "I love you".

***

Later that afternoon, after Tommy finished lunch at Chef Ho's Chinese restaurant, he saw the paper at the corner newsstand with the Sister Margaret case on the front page. He grabbed a copy and walked over to Bailey's Corner Pub.

He took a stool at the end of the bar in his favorite spot, ordered a Budweiser, and started to read Nunez's piece. 'Not bad kid, not bad at all,' he thought, smiling to himself, 'Glad I don't have to come tune you up.'

At about four in the afternoon Tommy was on his fourth Budweiser. He looked around the bar: The place had a decent crowd, not busy but every barstool was taken. The barmaid, Molly, a cute, perky, twenty-something was working the bar with three or four conversations going at the same time as she slung the drinks and kept everyone from going dry.

Molly was a good and attentive bartender, with sparkling green eyes, light red hair, and a sassy attitude, a definite plus for Baileys Corner as she knew how to work the bar and its regulars. Molly came to the end of the bar to check on Tommy, but then looked past him and spoke to someone behind him.

"Who are you with, honey?"

"No one," a young voice answered, "I'm lookin for him."

Tommy turned slightly on the stool and looked behind him to see a young boy of about twelve. He had short sandy blonde hair and a thousand yard stare. 'This is no Upper East Side prep school kid,' he thought to himself, 'this is a Yorkville Boy.'

"You lookin for me?" Tommy asked the boy.

"Yeah. You Tommy, right?"

"Who wants to know?"

"If you're Tommy, you need to go to Reif's."

"I need to go to Reif's?" Tommy asked.

"You heard me. And don't make him wait."

"Make who wait?" Tommy asked, but the young man gave him his blank stare, a slight smirk, then turned and walked out the door. Molly smiled at Tommy and gave a cute shrug.

"Give me a shot of Jameson please, Molly. I have to go see an old friend."

He threw back the shot of whiskey, put another twenty on top of the few bills that were already on the bar, and put his jacket on.

"Have a good day, kid. Talk to you soon."

"Bye Tommy," Molly replied, "will I see you later?"

"No, Molly, I don't think I'll be back again today."

"Okay, well I'm working till eight if you're thirsty," she said with the prettiest green eyes and a crooked smile.

"I don't think I'll be back tonight kid, but I will be soon," Tommy returned the smile. "Have a good night, love," and he stepped out of the bar.

Tommy walked over to Reif's Bar on 92nd Street, a place he had frequented regularly as a teenager. Now that he kept a low profile in the neighborhood and had disassociated himself from many of his old, less than savory friends, he hadn't been in Reif's for a good fifteen, maybe eighteen years.

As he approached the bar, Tommy saw the twelve year-old leaning against the brick wall outside, sharing a cigarette with a younger friend. They both eyed Tommy as he walked up and entered the bar.

He stopped inside the front door and scanned the room. It all looked the same, possibly a little cleaner than he remembered, but then he was a little cleaner these days himself.

An attractive blonde woman in her late forties turned from her seat at the bar. She broke out in a broad smile, showing a broken front tooth. "Holy shit! Look what the cat dragged in. As I live and breathe, it's Tommy Keane!" She stood up and opened her arms, beckoning Tommy to come give her a hug.

"Hey Anne Marie, how you doing, honey?" Tommy said as he gave her a long, hard hug.

"I'm doin great, Tommy, how's about you? You sure are looking good. You still a cop?"

"You're looking good yourself, Anne Marie. Yeah I'm still on the job."

"It is *so* good to see you, Tommy. Hey, let me introduce you to my friend Deirdre... Deirdre, this is Tommy, he used to be a regular around here. And quite the man in the neighborhood, weren't you, Tommy?" Both women smiled at him.

"Listen, Anne Marie, I'm here to see Terry. Is he here?"

"Is he here? Where else would he be? He's in the back, Tommy."

"Thanks dear," he motioned to the bartender, a thick-necked, red-faced, fat fellow of about fifty in a red plaid shirt "Back these two ladies up for me, will ya pal?" The bartender nodded as Tommy dropped a twenty onto the bar.

***

Tommy Keane and Terry Callahan had been best friends from kindergarten through the eleventh grade, when, at the age of seventeen, Terry was jumped in the bathroom of their high school. The assailants were a gang of black students who called themselves the Cigar Mob. Terry always had a knife in his pocket, and when he was knocked to the floor, he pulled it out and cut one of his attacker's Achilles' tendons, instantly dropping him to the floor. Terry then rose back up and plunged the knife into another attacker's chest three times.

The boy bled out while Terry returned to the teenager with the cut tendon and repeatedly stomped on him while the other two boys fled the scene. Terry, being seventeen, was held and charged as an adult. He spent three and a half years of a seven year sentence behind bars.

After Terry went away, Tommy got his GED and joined the army, becoming a paratrooper with the 82nd Airborne Division. Tommy did his four years in the service and whenever he came home he kept a low profile in the neighborhood.

Although the attack, and its consequences for Terry, had nothing to do with Tommy, Tommy always felt an inner guilt that he had somehow let his best friend down. That if he had only been there for him, the attack would never have happened, or maybe they would have gone away together.

Either way, Tommy always had a hole in his heart from losing the Terry he knew and loved as a boy. The one person he had shared everything in his childhood with was lost, and somehow Tommy's youth seemed lost after that as well.

Tommy walked toward the back of the pub and his eyes met those of his lifelong friend, Terry Callahan. Terry was roughly the same size as Tommy, but with more of a weight lifter's physique. He had short, cropped dirty-blonde hair, grey-blue eyes, and a pronounced scar over his left eye that went through his eyebrow and reappeared for about a quarter of an inch on his left cheek.

He had the look of a working man, a construction worker, or maybe a longshoreman from the 1950's. He was a handsome man with a solid build and, much like Tommy, he shared the noticeable trait of looking like he had always been a part of this neighborhood, and also as if he didn't belong here at all.

"Tommy," he said in his low voice. Terry never needed to raise his voice. The two men embraced in a long, strong hug.

"Good to see you, Tommy," Terry said as he took a step back.

"Good to see you, Terry."

Anne Marie was watching them and leaned over to whisper to Deirdre, "Look at them. TNT is what we used to call them, cause it was always Terry and Tommy. They were the best of friends back in the day."

Terry walked back to the corner where he had been sitting at a small, two-top high rise table, near the backdoor. He took his chair, with his back to the corner, and motioned for Tommy to join him. The bartender brought Terry a fresh beer.

"I hear you're back on 88th with your moms and workin in the 2-1?"

"You heard right," Tommy replied, "and I understand you're still runnin things around here and staying one step ahead of the law yourself?"

"Always," Terry took a swig from his bottle of beer. "You know I've always been too quick for them, Tommy." They both chuckled.

"What's up brother? Why did you call me here today? I know it's not because you miss me."

"I do miss ya, Tommy. You know I have for years. But I also know you can't hang out with a miscreant like me anymore. If some FBI fucker was to snap a photo of us together, poof, there goes your job and your pension, right?"

"Well, let's just say I'd have some explaining to do," Tommy replied. "So what's up, Terry?"

Terry rubbed his hand over the stubble on his chin and leaned back a little. "I know you picked up that scumbag Benny H for that nun murder... and I gotta tell you pal, you pinched the wrong punk. That Benny is no doubt a piece of shit, but he ain't capable of that. Believe me, I ain't a fan of his either, but I hate to see you make a mistake and nail the wrong guy. One, cause it's you, and two, cause that means the real killer is still runnin around out there."

"We got him on camera on the block, he's got a prior for assault on another priest, and his own girlfriend puts him at the scene. It's a pretty solid collar, Terry."

"You work a confession out of him?"

Tommy shook his head, "No, we didn't."

"You got prints or DNA, or any of that forensics shit you guys do these days?"

"Nothing back from the lab yet."

"Alright, so what you wanna bet I'm right and you got the wrong guy?"

"You know I never bet, Terry. You know something I don't?"

"You know what I know, Tommy? I know this neighborhood. I know every piece of shit criminal and every piece of shit junkie in this neighborhood. And I know that particular piece of shit Benny, Benny H, Benny Heroin--he ain't got the stones to do this. Don't get me wrong, he is a desperate low-life in the first degree, but what I heard he did, what I read he did in the papers... Nope, it don't fit. When I heard you were the one that scooped him up, I just felt I had to let you know--again, for you, not for him. I could care less if Benny H spends the rest of his pitiful life upstate, the neighborhood would be better off without him. But I'm tellin you, youse grabbed the wrong guy here."

Terry took another swig of his beer, and changed the subject, "Hey, how's your mother? I haven't seen her for a while. I understand she don't leave the house too often anymore. She feeling alright? And Caitlyn, how's she doin up there in college? Sienna right? Nice Catholic school. Funny, your daughter in a Catholic school... You hate all that church shit."

"Yeah, Ma is doin alright, Terry. She's getting a little loopy but she's doing alright. And Caitlyn is liking school so far. It's still really new to her but she likes it and likes her roommate... Listen, I appreciate your input on Benny Hirschle, I really do, but it's not my case, Terry. I was just there as backup. But I'll look a little deeper into it, and I'll let the arresting detective know to look a little deeper, too."

"Hey, I didn't tell you shit."

"Of course not, Terry, I'd never put your name in anything."

"Good man. Can I buy you a beer?"

"Sorry, Terry, I can't. I love you brother, but I got things I gotta do and hanging out in here isn't one of them."

"Yeah. I figured as much. I miss ya, Tommy."

"I miss you too, Terry. Keep your head down and your eyes open."

"Always," Terry replied as Tommy stood up and walked past the pool table towards the front door.

Tommy walked out of Reif's, despite the calls from Anne Marie to sit and drink, and once outside he walked straight back to Our Lady of Perpetual Hope. It was Sunday evening, the first day of his two days off.

Back at the school, Sister Claire let Tommy into Sister Margaret's office again, where he spent over three hours going over everything there was to go over. He sat perfectly still in an old oak office chair he put in place of Sister Margaret's chair, which still had dried blood on it, for at least half an hour just taking in what the room had to offer.

'Was Terry right?' he thought, 'What am I missing? What can I possibly be missing?'

Tommy sat, he looked, and he searched in silence, slowly and methodically looking at every inch of the room. But nothing jumped out at him; nothing was out of place or strange.

'There is always a clue, some piece of evidence,' he reminded himself, but there was nothing he could find to change anything that they knew. Benny was on film, Benny was a desperate junkie, Benny had a prior conviction for an attack on a priest, and Benny's girlfriend put him here herself. 'Fuck me, it's got to be him, we have to have the right guy,' he thought. 'But the evidence... it's still not there. It's still not enough. Fuck. Do we have the right guy?'

Chapter Sixteen

On Tuesday afternoon, Sergeant Browne walked into the 2-1 squad room with a cup of coffee, and a haggard look that said he had been in the office for some time now.

"Hey guys, we have some stuff back from the lab," he told Stein, handing him a file folder.

"Wow. Already?" asked Tommy, "I usually wait weeks, sometimes months, to get shit back from the lab."

"It's a high profile case, Tom. I'm sure the Arch Diocese or the Cardinal got a hold of the Mayor's Office and they got a hold of the lab and put the case in the front of the line," replied Sergeant Browne, slurping at his coffee.

"That never happens in the Bronx," Tommy replied.

"This ain't the Bronx," Browne added over his shoulder as he walked out the door.

The team all converged around Stein's desk to view the reports from the lab. Stein read them all thoroughly to himself and then cleared his throat to read the reports aloud.

"Fingerprints were positive, in that they were able to lift several, and one very good thumb print from the murder weapon, which was an OXO Good Grips kitchen knife, 13 inches long, with an eight inch long, inch and a half wide blade. However, the prints do not match our suspect."

"They don't match?" asked Colletti.

"That's right. The print doesn't belong to Benny Hirschle and there is no match on file or found, as of now." He continued reading, "As far as DNA goes, no blood was found anywhere in the room or outside of the room other than that of the victim. There were many hair samples discovered, of which none match our man Benny. A subsequent search of Benny and Sharon's apartment was ripe with DNA, none of which matched Sister Margaret. In other words, Benny didn't bring any physical evidence in the form of blood, hair, or fibers home with him.

"And here are two--ahem," Stein cleared his throat again, "here are two very interesting discoveries made by our friends downtown. The first is that Sister Margaret was killed by the first stab wound to the chest, which entered her heart and killed her almost instantaneously. This we sort of assumed at the scene and was affirmed by the ME because of the lack of excessive bleeding from the victim. Now, according to this report, because of the angle of the knife's entry to the chest and the damage to the clothing, it appears that the victims frock, or habit, or whatever her uniform is called, was already raised up and tucked into her collar, thereby exposing her body, prior to being stabbed to death. In other words, she was not killed then posed post-mortem. Most likely she was stabbed the first time exactly in the position and state of dress we initially found her in."

"What the fuck?" Colletti exclaimed.

"Wait," Stein said, "let me continue. There's more..."

"More?" Colletti exclaimed again.

"Shut up, Jimmy. Let him finish," Lieutenant Bricks interjected.

"Yes more," Stein continued. "There was also DNA found all over the victims' vulva."

"What the fuck is a vulva?" Colletti asked.

"Her vagina, stupid," Doyle responded.

"Yes, her vagina," Stein continued. "There was a large amount of saliva on, in, and around Sister Margaret's vagina."

The room hung in silence for about three seconds.

Lieutenant Bricks rubbed his face with both hands and let out a long breath. "And nothing? No prints or DNA belonging to Benny were found in the school, and no evidence from the body was found in the apartment?"

"Nothing here, Lu," Stein replied.

"Fuck," Lieutenant Bricks turned around and walked into his office. Another, louder "Fuck" echoed in the otherwise silent room.

"Fuck is right," said Colletti. "So wait, let me see if I'm getting this right. The Sister was killed while getting oral sex. Is that right? Is that what you're saying? And, and not by our guy Benny. As far as the DNA goes, it's not his spit in her Volvo?"

"That's right, Jimmy. That is what the evidence is saying. It's saying this case has taken a turn in a very different direction and we most likely got the wrong guy," Stein replied. "So, we have a whole new investigation here. Let's all go over this together in detail."

"Wow. What the fuck," Jimmy repeated, looking down in disbelief.

Sister Margaret

Chapter Seventeen

Tommy stared across the desk at Stein, who stared back for a few moments.

"What did we miss?" Stein asked.

"Fuck. I don't know," Tommy replied, "Maybe it was just too easy. Everything pointed to Benny right away, so maybe...so maybe somehow we overlooked something?"

Stein sighed and grumbled under his breath, tapping his pen against his desk.

"Actually, a contact, an old friend told me we had the wrong guy this weekend," Tommy said, "So I went back to the school yesterday...just in case."

Stein looked inquisitively over his glasses at Tommy, "A friend?" he asked.

"Yeah, a guy I've known for years, someone who's in tune with the neighborhood. He said it wasn't Benny, so I went back to see if there was anything we missed."

"Who is this guy? What does he know?"

Stein was a little taken aback by Tommy's casual confession. He really didn't know Tommy, and Tommy wasn't lead on this case, Stein was. Why would he be following up on it while off duty? And was there anything else that Tommy hadn't shared?

Stein took a deep breath and relaxed. 'He's not keeping anything from me,' he thought, 'He just wants to share facts, and right now he has none.' Somehow, he trusted Tommy was doing the right thing. He was working something out in his head about this case. It was true he didn't know a lot about Tommy, but over the last week of working with him and having heard of his reputation as a thorough, if not brilliant investigator, he had decided that Tommy was a decent man and a trustworthy detective. Hell, Stein actually liked him.

"Just an old friend from years ago. He doesn't have a thought on who did this, just that it wasn't Benny. Believe me, I wish he had told me more than that we were wrong. I wanted to believe Benny was our man, but I know this guy good, and I know he wouldn't have bothered if he didn't believe we were mistaken about Benny.

Both detectives sat for a few seconds in silence, and then Tommy stood up.

"Grab your jacket."

"What's up?" Stein asked while he stood up.

"C'mon, we're going back to the scene."

***

When they arrived at the school, Sister Claire looked slightly annoyed to see them again. She was polite and congenial, but had a look of tired exasperation on her face when they asked, once again, for entry to Sister Margaret's office.

After she unlocked the door both detectives carefully entered the office. Stein turned toward her at the threshold and said, "Thank you, Sister. We'll let you know when we're all finished up," and then slowly closed the door on her. The men stood still in front of the closed door and stared up at the four-foot crucifix behind Sister Margaret's desk.

Tommy spoke, "Okay, Mark, it's here. Something is here. We have most of the forensics back, thanks to our Mayor, or Police Commissioner, or Cardinal, or whoever. We have something there, a print or possibly some DNA, but whose? We have a nun, a woman of the cloth, apparently having a sexual relationship right here just moments--hell, maybe seconds--before or even *during* her murder."

Tommy exhaled loudly and ran his hands through his short hair. "The video shows us a convicted priest fighter on the block, coming and going just before and just after the murder took place, but we have to forget about him for now, Mark. We have to forget him because we have nothing more than coincidence. Forgive me, Mark, I'm thinking out loud to try and work this out..."

"No, keep going," Stein replied, "it's helping me also."

"We were all here. We saw the aftermath, and we all drew our own conclusions. We collected the evidence, the same evidence that is now pulling us in a different direction. Fuck. There is something here that we overlooked, so let's look at everything again. This is where it happened. What did we not notice before?"

They stood and looked around: The room was immaculately clean, except for the now-dried blood that still remained and the items the detectives themselves had disturbed during their searches.

They slowly walked around the small office, re-opened the file cabinets, re-searched the pockets of both the sweater and jacket that hung on the hooks on the wall.

Tommy picked up a photo album that was full of photos of students and faculty at the school. He leafed through it, page by page, and then placed it back on the shelf. Then he moved on to one of the yearbooks on the shelf. He paused, suddenly, and reached for the photo album again.

"Stein, open up that top right drawer and tell me what you see."

Stein opened the top right hand drawer of Sister Margaret's desk. There were pens, paper clips, rubber bands, and office supplies along with school papers and a few handwritten logs.

He picked up the pile of documents and fanned through it, and three photographs dropped to the desk. All three were school photos, professional portraits with a blue background, and each subject was a young girl in her early teens, wearing her blue plaid Catholic School uniform. The photos were so typical that they could have been taken yesterday or thirty years ago.

"You see those photos in with that other stuff?" Tommy asked.

"Yes I do," Stein replied, unsure where this was going.

"They came from this photo album, I think. The photos in the desk are the same size as the missing photos from this album. You see how the adhesive left an imprint? It would appear they are the only photos missing from this album."

"What are you thinking, Tommy?"

"I don't know."

Tommy separated the photos and laid them out on the desk.

"Mark, can you find Sister Claire and ask her to come in here, please?"

"What do you have, Tommy? What did you find?" Stein asked a second time.

"I don't know, but I want to ask her about these girls."

Stein nodded and left the office, returning a few minutes later with Sister Claire.

"Here, step into the hallway here, Sister," he ushered her out of the office. "I don't want the room to disturb you. I'm curious, Sister, do you know these girls?" Tommy asked, showing her the three photographs.

"Of course, Detective, they are all students here."

"Who are they please?"

"This is Heather, Heather O'Hearn, and this one, um this one is Claudia Aguilar. Her mother works here as well. And this one is Brianne Holtz."

"Thank you, dear. Do you know what grade they're each in? Better yet, do you have any paperwork, any kind of admission forms we could see?"

"Um yes, of course. Um, Heather and Claudia are in the ninth grade and Brianne is in the eighth, and they all should have files in those cabinets to the left of Sister Margaret's desk."

"Thank you so much, Sister Claire. Please stay close, we may have some more questions for you very soon," Tommy ended the conversation and then motioned Stein to reenter the office. He smiled at the Sister and slowly closed the door, leaving her behind in the hallway once more.

"These girls are all underage so we're going to have to bring them in with their parents to question them."

"You want to question these girls?" Stein asked, "What? Do you think these girls had something to do with this?"

"Listen, we have nothing in this room. Nothing stands out to me but these photos right now. They're... well, they're just odd to me, let's say. They're probably nothing, probably just photos of Sister Margaret's favorite students, or year-end gifts to a favorite teacher, but unfortunately we can't just ask these girls if that's the case. We're going to have to bring their parents in in order to have a simple conversation with them. I'm guessing all of them are about fourteen to fifteen. I don't know, Mark, it's just odd and well, we got nothing else."

"Alright, let's find out who these girls are, and what? Have them meet us at the Station House? Go to their homes or meet here or what? I'm going to say here is better, more comforting to both the girls and the parents," Stein said, answering his own question.

"Agreed," Tommy replied, "I'll see what I can find in these files."

"Very good. I'll call the Lu and let him know what we're doing."

"Cool," Tommy replied as he opened the file cabinet and started leafing through the folders.

Chapter Eighteen

Tommy and Stein quickly located and spoke to the parents of the three girls in the photos, and set up appointments for the next afternoon and evening. The meetings were to take place in a classroom in Our Lady of Perpetual Hope.

The first interview was at 3:20 pm with Claudia Aguilar and her mother, Irma Aguilar.

Stein began, "Hello ladies, thank you so much for helping us out today. I want you to know we're just going to ask you about Sister Margaret a little, okay? No one is in any sort of trouble here. And I want you to understand that you, of course, don't have to speak to us at all. We are just trying to find out who killed Sister Margaret, that's all we care about. Do you understand?"

Claudia nodded yes. She was a small, pretty girl with long dark brown hair and soulful brown eyes. She wore her hair straight, parted down the middle, with a small barrette clipped to the side near her temple.

Irma, Claudia's mother, stated in a heavy El Salvadoran accent, "Jes, we want to help. I don't think we know nothing but we want jou to catch deese evil mens that kill sweet Sister Margaret."

Stein continued, "You work here don't you Mrs. Aguilar?"

"Jes, I am the janitor. I work here for three, almost four years," Irma replied.

"And you, Claudia, you are in the ninth grade this year? And are what, fourteen years old?"

Claudia nodded with her head lowered, not making eye contact.

"Answer deese police," Irma said in a low but forceful tone.

"Yes," Claudia replied.

Stein continued asking simple questions about the day of the homicide: Had they seen anyone or anything suspicious? Had they heard anything the police may be interested in? Were there any rumors floating around amongst the students or the faculty that they thought the police should know?

This went on for about an hour, but nothing of interest came from the interview. Irma confidently answered "No" to just about every question related to anything being out of the ordinary on the day of the homicide. Claudia, who was quite shy, had only one-word answers for every question.

Both Detectives thanked the Aguilars for their time and escorted them to the classroom door.

Heather O'Hearn and her mother, Shelly O'Hearn, entered the classroom at 4:30 and sat down. Heather was pretty, very thin, and freckled, with dirty-blonde hair. She looked a couple years younger than her actual age of fourteen.

Shelly was also thin. She wore too much makeup, new but cheap-looking clothes, and a strong perfume that filled the room. She also looked much older than her rather young thirty-three years of age. She appeared to be annoyed at having been called in, and not a bit concerned about Sister Margaret.

The fact that a murder had occurred in her daughter's school did not seem to have rattled Shelly. She was unusually flirty under the circumstances, both detectives thought, and she mentioned on more than one occasion that her ex-husband was a cop in Queens, and that she had "always had a thing for cops."

Stein began the interview in the same way as the previous one that afternoon. He tried to make the ladies comfortable and began with the same basic questions the detectives had asked the Aguilars.

This time, however, the detectives directed the conversation to Heather. Although Heather was not nearly as shy as Claudia, she had nothing of any value to say. She gave mostly one-word answers, with the exception of comments like "why am I even here?," "Like none of this has anything to do with me other than my mother makes me go to this school," and "Why would you even group me with that weird girl that just left? We don't even know each other."

The O'Hearns' interview went on for about fifty minutes before the detectives decided it was going nowhere. Again they thanked the ladies for their time and let them leave. As they left the room Shelly turned in the doorway and looked Tommy straight in the eyes.

"Glad to be of service, Detectives. You know where to find me if you need anything else. Anything. I hope you won't hesitate to call."

Stein smiled at Tommy when they were alone again, "Anything," Stein repeated.

Tommy smiled and shook his head.

Sister Margaret

At 5:46, Mr. Steven Holtz entered the room, alone, for the interview. He was a slight, well-dressed man of forty-four years of age, who worked for Morgan Stanley. He was trying to be confident but was obviously nervous.

"I wanted to ask, gentlemen, what this is all about, before I bring my wife and daughter in. I know this is about Sister Margaret, I know that, but I am concerned why my daughter Brianne has been singled out for questioning and if, if I need, or we need, a lawyer present for this?" Mr. Holtz asked.

"Come on in and sit down, Mr. Holtz. We totally understand your concern. I want you to know that your daughter Brianne is in no way in trouble or a suspect of any sort. I also want you to know that neither you nor she has to talk to us at all, and you most certainly may ask to have an attorney present if you'd like to. Brianne also has not been singled out, we are just asking as many people as possible about this case so we can get to the bottom of it," Stein replied.

"I thought you already had her killer. I saw it on the news, and read all about it in the paper, you got the guy, no? Some junkie with an axe to grind against the church, right?" Mr. Holtz asked.

"Well, we made an arrest, yes, but there are still a lot of loose ends we have to tie up before we go to trial, Mr. Holtz. I'm sure you understand that," Tommy replied.

"Yes, yes I understand. Well I guess it's okay if you ask Brianne some questions."

Steven Holtz stood up and went to open the door. He called his wife and daughter in, both of whom were also well-dressed and quite attractive. Although Brianne was much more talkative, forthcoming, and downright charming than her peers, she was no more helpful than they had been.

Stein and Tommy thanked the family for coming in, and once they had left the room, they both let out large mournful sighs.

"So, what you think?" Tommy asked.

Stein replied, "I think we are in a spot here, Detective. I don't know what your gut told you about those photos, and I'm not second-guessing you, but I don't think we have anything here. Seems like an empty, unfulfilling day and I'm more at a loss now than I was when we found out Benny isn't our man. You?"

"Yeah this is a tough one, but I don't have to tell you, Stein, there *is* something here. There's something either we overlooked, or that is right in our hands that we aren't seeing, or quite possibly something is staring us right in the face and smiling while we run around in circles," Tommy let out another deep sigh. "I'm hungry. What you say we get some Italian Village while we go over everything again?"

The two detectives stood up and left the classroom, closing the door. Stein pulled his coat on as they walked down the hall.

"Doreen says you eat for free there, is that true? She says you're like a celebrity when you walk in the place. How is it the pizza man treats you like a movie star and old friends show up out of nowhere to tell you we arrested the wrong man before the lab results are even back, Tommy?" Stein asked with his inquisitive look.

"Nothing is ever free, Mark. But what can I say... I'm an interesting man."

"No doubt," Stein replied.

Sister Margaret

Chapter Nineteen

The two detectives sat in the Italian Village Pizzeria staring across the table at one another, just as they had done back at the Station House when their shift had started. Even after re-visiting the crime scene and interviewing the girls and their parents, they had nothing more to go on.

"What are we missing?" Tommy asked out loud, both to Stein and himself as he bit into a slice of pizza.

"I don't think it's Benny," Stein replied, "I think we made a solid arrest there with what we had to go on, but I'm certain he is no longer the guy we're looking for here. Fuck I've looked at this every way I can. I just don't know where else to go or what else we can look for."

Tommy wiped the pizza sauce from the side of his mouth. "Let's head back to the Station and see if anything else has come in. Maybe Doreen and Jimmy have something, or God-willing, some positive on that print or DNA?"

When they arrived back at the Station, the rest of the squad had left for the day but two members of the other team were in. Detective Kehoe shouted to them as they entered the room.

"Hey Stein, Doyle left you a note and a memory stick of some security videos she and Colletti collected for you."

"Thanks, Kehoe. How's your wife, she feeling better?" Stein replied.

"Much better, thanks."

Stein pulled his chair out and sat at his desk to read the note from Doreen Doyle, which read:

"Hey Mark, we saved everything from the morning of Sister Margaret's murder on this drive. Jimmy and I went over all of it a few times. Combined, there is hours of stuff on here. Nothing really stood out to us, but please take a look for yourself. I don't want to miss anything... See you in the morning –D

P.S. also was told that your boy Benny took a beating in Rikers, nothing serious just a broken nose."

"Supposedly Benny got a beat down in Rikers, according to Doreen. She left some footage here from the cameras they collected. I'm going to go through it now. Do you want to sit, or you heading home for the night?" Stein asked Tommy.

"Ha! Well he may not be our man for this homicide, but I'm sure he had that broken nose coming to him. Yeah I definitely want to stay, four eyes are always better than two. Plug it in."

Tommy grabbed a chair and rolled it over to Stein's desk and the two detectives sat side by side in front of the computer, reviewing what Doyle and Colletti had collected. All in all, it took four hours to go over each of the cameras. About an hour into the footage, Tommy made a mental note of the video from one of the cameras: Benny Hirschle walking past the camera in both directions at 6:02 in the morning and 6:18 in the morning.

When all of the footage had been played, he asked Stein, "What did you see?"

"Tommy, my eyes are a blur after watching all this shit. I have to say, nothing unusual. The only thing I really noticed was Benny Hirschle, but we knew we would see him and we knew he would come and go in both directions. You?"

"Go back to Camera Two, and to 6:04 time... There... right there. Who is that?" Tommy asked.

"Ahh looks like Irma the janitor, Claudia, and another student. A little early to be going to school, but maybe they all go together in the morning because Irma has to go to work. Interesting though... and look it's a couple minutes after Benny walks by the same location and a few minutes before he returns. So it's all in the same time frame that we pegged Benny for... So, what? You think Irma or Claudia had something to do with this now?" Stein asked.

"Man, I don't know. I really don't know. After meeting them it seems unlikely, near-impossible, but it does fit the time frame. I really didn't get the feel that either of them was capable of this, but hey, you never know, I guess. This is one hell of a mystery and here is a new little piece that just seems out of the ordinary. What say we go see these ladies again in the morning?"

"Alright," Stein replied, "I don't see them as our suspects, but it couldn't hurt. At the very least they were there, or close to there, when it happened. Maybe, just maybe they remember something that points us in the right direction."

"Okay, tomorrow morning. Meet you here and we'll head back over to the school first thing."

Both detectives signed out and headed to their respective homes.

Sister Margaret

***

At 7:00 am the next morning Tommy walked into the squad room just in time to see Stein opening up his beat-up briefcase and picking out the tie he would wear for the day.

"Good morning, Detective. How ya feeling this morning? You get a good night's sleep?" Tommy asked.

"Morning, Tommy, and no, not much at all. Between this case and my wife's snoring, I may have gotten two hours total shut eye. But what's a man to do? I love her too much to sleep in the other room."

Stein got to his feet and put his overcoat on as Charice Tate walked into the room, carrying a stack of files and paperwork.

"Ooooh baby, you two men better keep an eye out for the Captain today! He's on the warpath baby, and he ain't too happy with you two for grabbin the wrong guy fo that nun murder. No sir he ain't too happy at all. I'd keep a low profile if my name was Stein or Keane in this House. Yes sir I sho would, at least until you catch the real killer," she reported dramatically, as she walked to Sergeant Browne's office to drop off more paperwork.

"What say we do keep a low profile and head out, Mark?" Tommy asked.

"Right behind you," Stein replied.

***

They arrived at the school at 7:33, a little less than an hour before the students were to arrive, and went straight to the main office on the first floor to speak with Sister Claire. They asked if Irma and Claudia were in yet, and if there was a room they could use for an hour or so to speak with them again. Sister Claire said nothing, but nodded and quietly led them to the small Nurse's Office, adjacent to the room they were in.

Tommy and Stein sat in the small, sterile office and waited for Irma and Claudia to arrive. In a matter of minutes the ladies knocked on the door jamb. Both had surprised looks on their faces and seemed uneasy to find the detectives waiting for them.

"Good morning, Detectives," Irma Aguilar said as she entered the office. Claudia remained silent, and again avoided eye contact with the men.

"Good morning," both detectives replied in near unison.

"Please sit down. We just had a few more questions to ask you about the day we lost Sister Margaret," Stein said in a slow, comforting voice.

"Jes, jes of course," Irma Aguilar responded, "anything, please anything."

Tommy opened up a manila folder and showed the women a photo of Benny Hirschle, "Have either of you ladies seen this man before? Do either of you know him?"

Both looked at the photo intently for a moment.

"No, I don't think so," Irma replied, shaking her head.

"No sirs, I don't know that man," Claudia added quietly.

"Okay," Stein continued, "Do you usually come to school at this hour?"

"Que?" asked Irma.

"Early, do you always come to school so early?" Stein repeated the question.

"Oh jes always early, before classes, so everything is ready for the students and the Sisters," Irma explained, nodding emphatically.

"And you as well, Claudia?"

"Yes sir, we come and help our mother with her job before and after school."

"We? You mean the other girl we saw you with on the day Sister Margaret died?"

"Yes, my sister Eva always comes with us," Claudia replied. Then she paused and asked, "You saw us coming to school that day?"

"We have a security video that shows you and your mother, and I suppose your sister Eva, as well as that man we just showed you, heading towards the school that morning. Now where is your sister today?" Stein asked, a bit surprised, and now slightly annoyed that he hadn't known there was a sister.

"Eva is here," Irma replied.

"She's on the third floor right now making sure everything is ready," said Claudia.

"Why haven't we met Eva?" asked Stein.

"I dunno? You asked only to meet us," Irma replied.

"Yes, we only asked to meet with Claudia and her guardian originally. That's because we had no idea there was another sibling, or that she was on the surveillance video," Tommy said.

"That's right," Stein agreed. "Tom, can you ask Sister Claire, or one of the other ladies, to go get Eva for us?"

"Absolutely," Tommy replied as he stood up.

Stein continued to ask Irma and Claudia details about the morning of Sister Margaret's homicide, while Tommy returned to the main office to ask one of the other nuns to retrieve Eva from the third floor.

Sister Sarah headed upstairs, and Tommy rejoined Stein, Irma, and Claudia in the Nurse's Office. Stein was still conducting a cursory interview--simple questions pertaining to the morning of the crime. He asked about people they may have passed on the street, about staff and other students in the school and so on, but nothing stood out as unusual to either detective. Tommy even got a smile out of Claudia when he mentioned how much of a lady she was in comparison to some of her other classmates. He didn't mention Heather by name but Claudia guessed at his reference.

After a few minutes there was a knock at the door.

"Come in," Stein said. Sister Sarah opened the door, smiled gently at Irma and Claudia, and asked the detectives to step outside.

In the hall Sister Sarah spoke in a hushed tone, "I did as you asked, Officer. I went and found Eva, but when I told her you were downstairs wanting to speak with her she ran like a shot down the stairs and out the door. I have no idea which direction she went."

Both detectives looked at each other and immediately headed for the front door. "You go east and I'll go west," Tommy shouted as they ran outside to the sidewalk.

Tommy and Stein made it to their respective corners, only to find dozens of young girls approaching the block from every direction, all at the same time and all in the same plaid uniform.

"Eva Aguilar!" Stein shouted, "Have any of you girls seen Eva Aguilar?" The girls all looked at him as if he were a mad man, or worse.

Tommy was equally overcome. Rather than yelling out, he took a deep breath, stood still and looked around methodically for anyone who was heading in the opposite direction of the crowd. He had no luck. He stood for another few minutes then took another breath and headed back towards the school.

As he approached the front entrance he radioed Stein to see if he had been more successful. Stein responded, "Negative," and the men agreed to reconvene on the front steps.

"Interesting development," Stein remarked, gasping for breath as he approached Tommy, who was waiting calmly at the door. "I need to take better care of myself. I ran half a block and I can't breathe. She would've kicked my ass if I had caught her!"

Tommy got on his radio, "Central, 2-1 Squad looking for a female, Hispanic, dark hair, fifteen to eighteen years of age, grey and blue Catholic School girl's uniform, vicinity of East 93rd."

"Ain't we all," came over the air from an unknown cop on patrol.

"No unauthorized transmissions," Central replied, then, "Copy that 2-1 Squad." The official voice repeated the description and sent out the call for assistance to "all available units."

Tommy and Stein exchanged a look and walked back into the school to rejoin the Aguilars in the Nurse's Office.

"How you wanna handle this?" Tommy asked Stein in a low voice.

"Cool, Tom, let's go at it cool. I don't think they know what just happened."

"I agree," Tommy replied.

They stopped outside the door and took a second to compose themselves.

"They can't seem to find her on the third floor," Stein said, as casually as he could, when they entered the room.

Both women looked puzzled--not alarmed so much as confused.

"We have Sister Sarah looking for her right now, but in the meantime, why don't the both of you tell me about Eva, since we haven't met her yet," Stein continued.

"I'm going to step outside for a moment," Tommy said to Stein pointing to his radio, "Just a minute."

Stein nodded and began to talk in a quiet, comforting manner to Irma and Claudia, asking simple questions about Eva starting with her age and grade.

About ten minutes had passed when Tommy heard the radio transmission, "2-1 Charlie Central. We have possible school girl on 95th and Lex fitting description from 2-1 Squad. Please advise."

"10-4, 2-1 Charlie," Central replied, "2-1 Squad you on the air? 2-1 Charlie has possible female on 9-5 and Lexington."

"2-1 Squad. Have 2-1 Charlie ask if her name is Eva."

"2-1 Charlie copy. Yes Central, this female's name is Eva."

"2-1 Squad copy. Central, please have 2-1 Charlie bring female to the Station House forthwith and await our arrival."

"2-1 Charlie, you copy?"

"2-1 Charlie copy... En route."

"10-4, 2-1 Charlie."

"2-1 Squad. Thank you Central and 2-1 Charlie."

"10-4."

Tommy opened the door, and motioned with his head for Stein to join him in the hallway.

"2-1 Charlie picked her up on 95ᵗʰ. They're taking her to the Station. You wanna bring these two with us and have a little family reunion, see what's going on here?" Tommy asked.

"Yes, I think that's where we're at. Listen, get ahold of Doyle," Stein added, "we may want a woman with us."

"I agree. I'll call her now. So what you think? You liking Eva for this?"

"Too early to tell, but she wouldn't bolt out of here for no reason."

"My thoughts exactly."

Chapter Twenty

Tommy, Stein, Irma, and Claudia all arrived at the Station House together and found Doreen Doyle and Jimmy Colletti waiting outside the entrance to the building.

"Jimmy, come on over here," Stein waved to Colletti. "Do me a favor and keep an eye on these two for a second?" He motioned to Irma and Claudia who stood nervously on the sidewalk next to the detectives' car.

"Of course," Jimmy replied.

Stein and Tommy walked over to Doyle, and Stein began, "Did Charlie bring in a young girl?"

Doreen responded, "Yeah, they have her up in the Muster Room."

"Okay good. Take her to the Squad Room, please. We're going to follow with her mother and see if she can answer some questions for us. I, we think she may have something to do with this. She ran from the school when she heard we wanted to talk to her. And, well, due to the nature of all this, and this girl's age, I think we'll have you interview her-- or at least start the interview to feel her out. Maybe it will be easier for her to talk to a young woman like yourself as opposed to an old dinosaur like me."

"Will do, anything to help... Mark, do you really think that little girl had something to do with this?" Doyle replied.

"I don't know, but it's certainly possible. And Doreen, be nice to her. Go slow and easy. If this is actually our girl she needs to feel you're a friend," Stein explained.

"I understand," Doyle replied.

He turned to Tommy, "What do you say we have Colletti sit with Claudia in the Muster Room and bring Irma upstairs to see if we can get some answers from Eva. We'll have Doyle with us for the feminine touch. I'm thinking there may be some sensitive subjects here that may be better handled female to female."

"I agree, I think you are right on point there," Tommy replied.

***

Tommy and Stein entered the Station House with Irma and Claudia Aguilar. As they headed for the steps Captain Peleggi stuck his head out of his office and loudly exclaimed, "Stein! Keane! My office now!"

Tommy replied, "Not now, Captain," as they began climbing the steps to the second floor Squad Room.

Captain Peleggi, in disbelief, repeated, "My office *now*, Detectives!"

Tommy turned to him from the third step of the stairs and, with a look of ice, stared Captain Peleggi in the eyes. In a low but very firm voice he replied again, "Not now, Captain," and proceeded to follow Stein and Irma up the stairs.

Captain Peleggi looked over the desk at Sergeant Ruffalo, who was looking down intently at his log book, then over to the Desk Officer at reception, who also had his eyes averted, apparently absorbed in paperwork. Peleggi stepped back in his office and slammed the door.

The three entered the squad room and found a teary-eyed Eva sitting at Doyle's desk. Doyle sat on the desk next to her, expectantly.

Irma rushed to her daughter, "Mi Amore mi amore, que est mal?" she asked.

"Irma, Mrs. Aguilar, may we speak with your daughter please? We need to speak to Eva now, okay?" Stein asked.

"Si si, jes of course," she replied, nodding her head at the detectives but looking increasingly worried.

"Eva, we have some questions to ask you. They are very important questions, dear. I know you're afraid, and I think I know why you're afraid, but please understand we are not here to hurt you. May we speak freely?" Stein asked in a soft, almost paternal fashion.

Eva nodded yes.

Tommy knelt next to her and quietly spoke, "Eva, I have a daughter about your age, and my partner here, Mark, has one a little older than you as well. I think we know why you ran from us. Would you like to talk to us or our friend Doreen here?" He asked, pointing up at Doreen.

Eva looked up and slowly pointed to Doreen.

"Doreen, would you like to go into the interview room for some privacy with Eva here?" Stein asked.

"Yes, yes I think that would be fine. Would you like something to drink, Eva?" Doyle asked.

Eva slowly shook her head no.

"Okay honey, come with me. It's nice and private in here," Doreen stood aside as Eva stood up shakily, and then she led the girl to the interview room.

Tommy brought Irma a cup of coffee and told her it might be a while. Then he joined Stein in the viewing room where they could observe Doyle's interview with Eva.

Doreen Doyle invited Eva to sit down. Then she moved her own chair halfway around the table so that the two young women were sitting next to one another. She raised her arm slowly and placed her right hand on Eva's left shoulder gently.

"Eva..." she began, "Eva, I know you know why you are here, honey. I want you to know we also know that Sister Margaret had some secrets, some pretty dark and shameful secrets that no one knew about. Well, no one other than you." Eva took a very deep breath at that moment, and Doyle continued, "I want you to know, Eva, that Detective Stein and Detective Keane and I are not here to hurt you, okay? We are just searching for the truth. Do you understand? Look at me, honey."

Eva looked up from the table into Doyle's eyes.

"We know Eva, we know. We have fingerprints and we have DNA. Do you know what DNA is, honey?" Eva nodded yes.

"Okay so you know we know. What we want, what we want and what we really need though, Eva, is for you to tell us the truth about what happened, and why it happened. Can you do that, honey? Eva, can you tell us your side of this story?"

Eva put her head down and shook it slowly, wrapping her arms around herself. Doreen looked at this young girl, who looked even younger in her Catholic School uniform, and sighed.

"Eva, I know it's scary when someone of authority betrays your trust," Eva seemed to shrink into herself more. "I know this and I am not going to betray you. Can you trust me? Can you tell me the truth?"

Eva continued to sit with her head down, holding herself. Doyle continued to speak with her calmly and soothingly for another half an hour, but Eva refused to look at her or speak a word. Finally, Doreen sighed and stood up.

"Okay honey, I'm going to go get you a soda, okay? I'll be right back." She left the room and quietly shut the door behind her, leaving Eva alone. She walked around to the other side of the room and met Stein and Keane where they stood watching.

"What do you think?"

"I think she has a story to tell," Tommy responded. He looked back through the mirror at Eva. She had placed her head down on her arms and was sobbing. "Grab her a soda, Doreen, and head back in. Looks like her defenses may be starting to weaken."

Doreen nodded and started to walk away, then she stopped and turned back to the detectives, "It's days like today when I ask myself why I took this job." She bought a Coke from the machines and made her way back to the interview room.

Eva was still sobbing with her head down when Doreen came back in. She placed the can of soda on the table, pulled her chair even closer to Eva and sat down. Then she leaned over and hugged her firmly and whispered, "It's going to be alright, honey. Let it out, it's going to be alright."

Sister Margaret

Eva picked her head up and looked into Doreen's eyes. Then she began to tell her story.

It had started in the beginning of Eva's second year at Our Lady of Perpetual Hope. Sister Margaret had taken a special liking to Eva, who was fifteen at the time, and began asking her to help in the office--simple cleaning and clerical tasks.

Eva, who was a below-average student, had trouble keeping her grades up, so Sister Margaret allowed her to do work for the school for extra credit. At the time, Mrs. Aguilar was a single mother and an undocumented immigrant, but her church had helped her obtain a job at the school. Shortly after, with the help of the school and the sponsorship of Sister Margaret, she received her green card. Eva's sense of gratitude and respect for her teacher and principal only grew stronger after that.

Sister Margaret had always been very kind to Eva. She often surprised her with gifts: new clothing, sweets, and occasionally small sums of money for helping her and the school. One afternoon she asked Eva to stay late and come to her apartment in the rectory--an increasingly common request-- and Eva immediately agreed.

She had no real friends at the school, and she very much liked that Sister Margaret had taken an interest in her. That Sister Margaret always had a soda and a packet of Ring Dings waiting for her, in addition to the gifts of money and clothing, only added to her affection towards the nun. She felt deeply indebted to her.

On this particular afternoon though, she asked Eva to do something different. After they had finished addressing invitations for an upcoming fundraiser, Sister Margaret asked Eva to shave her legs for her. She laughed lightly and said, "It always comes out better when someone else does it." Eva agreed, and although she felt strange, she did it without much hesitation. Sister Margaret stood in front of a full length mirror and watched as Eva delicately smoothed the shaving cream on each leg and then slowly and carefully shaved it off.

Once her legs were wiped clean Sister Margaret sat down in a chair in her bedroom and spread her legs. She directed Eva to continue to shave around her entire "private area." Eva's heart was in her throat, but she continued to follow Sister Margaret's instructions until the job was done. When she was finished, Sister Margaret sent her home.

Eva confessed that this scenario occurred three more times, but during the third incident, Sister Margaret asked her to lick her on her "private spot." Eva was mortified, but Sister Margaret insisted it was perfectly normal. She told Eva it was okay with God because it was not really sex; it was just like kissing people you loved. Sister Margaret placed her hand very gently on the back of Eva's head and guided her between her legs, where she slowly began to do as Sister Margaret instructed.

Eva stopped crying then, and continued with her story in a monotone voice, now separate from her emotions.

After that day, Eva explained, Sister Margaret had Eva visit her apartment or her office in the school three or four, sometimes five times a week. On one occasion, Eva tried to protest.

She told Sister Margaret that she could not continue these visits and Sister Margaret quietly but very firmly replied, "We all have to work here, Eva, we all have jobs to do. I do mine, the instructors do theirs, and your mother does hers. This is now your job, Eva. You wouldn't want your mother to lose hers, would you?"

These one-on-one instructional sessions, as the sister called them, continued for about eighteen months, Eva explained. Eva would meet Sister Margaret in her apartment after school, or in her office early before class began.

Often, Sister Margaret would lean a photograph of another girl up against her desk lamp and gaze upon it while Eva "did her job"--Heather and Brianne were two of her favorites.

Eva stopped her monologue and took a few deep breaths, shuddering to herself. She looked at Doreen who nodded to her that it was okay to continue.

About six weeks prior to Sister Margaret's murder, Eva stood up from her position on the floor and, while wiping her mouth after doing her job, she saw something that made her heart stop. It was a five by seven photo of her little sister, Claudia. She immediately looked away, saying nothing, and then rushed off to class.

Later that same week she saw Sister Margaret speaking to Claudia in the courtyard. They were both laughing and seemed to be sharing a private joke. Fear, an overwhelming fear, rushed over Eva. She kept a constant eye on her younger sister while they were at school, and watched for Sister Margaret as well. She became paranoid. She couldn't bear the thought of the sister looking at Claudia's photo while she did her job, but moreover she couldn't bear the thought of Claudia being forced into the same situation she was in. No, never Claudia.

The fear and pressure continued to build inside of Eva for the next few weeks. She could barely focus in school, and was always on edge at home. There was no one she could talk to, and no end in sight. Eva began to feel trapped by shame and despair.

Then, very early one morning, before any of the students or much of the staff had arrived, Eva went to Sister Margaret's office and asked if she could do her job now because she had a lot of things to do for her mother after school. Sister Margaret seemed happy, even flattered that Eva had come to her. She had never *asked* to do her job before.

Eva knelt down in front of Sister Margaret, who pulled her skirt up and neatly tucked it into her neckline and then sat back in her chair. She had a satisfied smile on her face as she enjoyed Eva's thorough, attentive licking. Eva continued her job while her mind was racing. She thought about how easy it would be to finish and go back to class. The day would continue like normal, no one would know a thing.

She was about to back out of her plan, when an image of Sister Margaret laughing with Claudia in the courtyard flashed through her mind. Her fear instantly turned to rage. She pulled out the kitchen knife she had brought from home and abruptly, without a thought, shoved it deep into Sister Margaret's chest.

Eva pushed the knife down until the handle met skin, running the blade straight through the sister's heart. She knew she was dead almost instantly. Then, Eva removed the knife and slashed the sister across her naked stomach, and again from her crotch up to her sternum. Finally, she plunged the knife deep into Sister Margaret's heart, where she left it.

Eva stood there silently for a few seconds. The rage was gone, but she didn't feel panicked at all. She felt rather relieved, and was in fact surprised to find that she wasn't covered in blood.

Eva told Doreen that she then stepped away from the desk and looked up at the four-foot tall crucifix that hung on the wall behind Sister Margaret's chair. She made the sign of the cross and then walked to the door, where she stuck her head out to make sure no one was in the hallway. Two doors down was the girls' room, where she quickly tiptoed and washed her hands.

She cuffed her sleeves to hide the small splatter of blood on her shirt, and looked at herself in the mirror. She couldn't believe she had actually done it. She breathed deeply, and realized she felt no guilt. In fact, she didn't feel much fear either, just a deep sense of satisfaction and righteousness.

But now almost two weeks later, sitting in the interview room with the nice officer, she was racked with emotion. It had all been her secret. No one--not a soul--knew it was Eva until now. Eva had no friends to confide in and she could never have told Claudia or her mother. But here in this small grey room with a kind-eyed detective she had just met, somehow it all came out. She spilled everything, simply because Doreen Doyle had said, "Can you tell us your side of the story?"

Chapter Twenty-One

And just like that, it was over. After two long weeks of investigation, the 2-1 Detective Squad had their man, which in the homicide case of Sister Margaret turned out to be a sixteen year-old girl. The City of New York was no longer threatened by an unknown maniac in search of a fresh body to carve.

There turned out to be no Satanist cult members, no ISIS terror cell, no junkie avenger. There was only a broken tenth grader, who had been abused by someone she trusted and was determined not to let her little sister become the next victim.

The investigation of Sister Margaret became one of those cases all detectives share--an exhausting ordeal without the final satisfaction of catching the perpetrator. In the end, the truth was much sadder and much more sinister than Sister Margaret's murder itself.

The squad room took on a somber and morose atmosphere once word of Eva's confession arose. Outside the interview room, Doyle gave Eva one last reassuring look and then stepped aside so Stein could bring her downstairs to the processing room. Meanwhile, Tommy called the Assistant District Attorney handling the case to let her know what had developed.

He informed the ADA, Amy Stekker, that they were presently booking the perpetrator and they would be in to see her in a few hours.

When he hung up, Tommy excused himself and stepped out of the squad room. He walked to the stairwell and sat down on the top step. He put his head down and ran his fingers through his hair, took a deep breath and then pulled his wallet out of his pocket. He quickly shuffled through some business cards to find the number he was looking for. Tommy took out his cell phone, then took another deep breath and dialed.

"Gil Nunez," was the answer on the phone.

"Hey, Gil. It's Tommy Keane."

"Detective Keane?" he repeated, surprised.

"Yes, I have a story you're going to want. It's an important story and it needs to be told right. Do you understand that? It needs to be told right. I will be very unhappy if it's not told properly. I'm calling you cause I think you're a decent guy, but if you fuck up this story, well… sorry. I'm sorry, Gil. You won't fuck up this story."

"Uh… Yes. Of course. Of course I'll tell it exactly the way you give it to me. I promise."

"Listen, I have a few hours work ahead of me still. I'm going to call you later so be sure you're available. We'll meet at The Globe on 23rd Street. Do you know the place?"

"No I don't, but I can find it."

"I have no idea when I'll be done, but when I am I'll let you know I'm on the way. Keep yourself available."

"Yes sir. I will, Detective."

"And don't say nothing to nobody else. This is between you and me and the rest of the city when you go to press tomorrow morning."

"Of course."

Tommy stepped back into the squad room and scanned the small cramped office: Stein was at his computer typing away; Colletti was on one knee next to Eva's mother Irma, holding a cup of coffee for her in one hand while his other rested gently on her shoulder. He consoled her as she wept almost silently. Doreen Doyle stood stoic yet visibly disheartened as she stood looking at Eva, shaking in Stein's chair. Eva stared at the wall in front of her, almost expressionless. Her small body shuddered but showed no sign of distress aside from the remnants of dried tears that trailed down her cheeks.

**

The night's work came to an end. The case, including the evidence and the confession of Eva Aguilar had been given to Assistant District Attorney Amy Stekker, who was very sympathetic to Eva's situation. ADA Stekker still had to do her job and present this case before the courts to be judged, and she would do her best to represent Eva fairly. For now, Eva was in custody, and Irma and Claudia were taken home by Doyle and Colletti.

As they were signing out for the night, Stein asked Tommy if he'd like a drink, but Tommy declined. "Thank you, Mark, but not tonight my friend. I actually have a date already that I'm very, very late for."

"Okay, Tommy. Fair enough. I'll see you tomorrow."

As Tommy walked to the corner and hailed a cab, he sent a text to Gil Nunez that he was on his way to meet him at the Globe. In the taxi on the way down, Tommy asked himself what he was doing--calling a reporter to tell him about a case that had not even gone to arraignment yet?

Tommy hated the media, but he felt this guy Gil was on the level. 'Maybe,' he thought to himself, 'this one can be trusted to do the right thing.' Tommy's hope was that Nunez could be a means to tell Eva's crucial story.

He needed Eva's side of the case to be told properly; he wanted to make sure pressure was put on the DA's office to see her as the victim, and to ensure that the Mayor's office and the Church saw Eva as a victim who acted in self-defense, and out of protection of her sister.

As Tommy's cab pulled up across the street from the bar, he saw Nunez outside waiting for him. He crossed the street to the entrance and they exchanged a firm handshake and stepped inside.

The two men sat alone at a back table where Tommy laid out the entire story, from the very beginning on the morning of the murder, through the arrest of Benny Hirschle, to its finality of Eva Aguilar's confession.

"Wow," Gil Nunez said in a low and truly astonished voice, "this could be a best-selling novel."

"Yeah, well, sadly there's nothing novel about this, Gil. This is a young girl's life. And I need you, she needs you, to do the right thing. Eva needs you to tell this story in its entirety. Be her champion and show the city that she has been the victim all along. Write this better than anything you have ever written before."

"I will. I understand what you want, Detective," Gil replied, "I get it."

Tommy stood and put out his hand.

"Thank you."

Gil looked up at him. He knew he had just received the scoop of a lifetime and he thought, 'This man is thanking me?' He grasped Detective Keane's outstretched hand.

"No, Detective Keane, thank you. Thank you for your trust, and your honesty. And thank you, sir, for doing this for Eva. I know she will never know it was you who told me her story, so let me thank you for her."

"I don't need any thanks, kid. Just do a good fucking job," Tommy replied still holding Gil's hand.

***

The following morning Tommy got up four minutes before the alarm was to sound, in his dark room at his mother's place on 88th Street. He rolled out of bed and did his fifty push-ups, got dressed, kissed his mother on the way out the door, and stepped outside, looking left and then right, scanning the block as he exited the building. It was a brisk, windy morning but the sun shone bright while he walked to the Precinct, picking up a spread of bagels, butter and cream cheese along the way.

The Station House was quiet as he made his way up to the empty squad room. He neatly laid out the bagels and condiments on a table, emptied the old coffee from the pot and started brewing a fresh batch. He had fixed himself an onion bagel with butter and was opening the bottle of orange juice he had bought for himself when Charice walked into the room, a stack of files in hand.

"Oooooh! Ooooh weee, baby, you got some reading to do to-day! You see the paper this morning, honey? Front page, baby. And it's a good article too. Tells a good story, sounds to me like that nun got what she had comin. That's what it sounds like to me! What you think, honey? You think she deserved a knife in the chest?" Charice exclaimed.

"Well, Charice, let's just say with the evidence being what it is, she got what she asked for," Tommy replied.

"I think you right, Detective. She got what she asked for, ha! She got what she asked for."

Stein entered the room while Charice handed out more papers. "Bagels, ah," he said, as he poured himself a cup of coffee and smeared cream cheese across a sesame seed bagel.

"You see the paper today, Detective?" Charice asked.

"Yes I did, Charice. Saw something on TV this morning as well...Amazing story, so much detail. I wonder how the reporter was able to uncover so much so quickly," Stein replied as he sat at his desk across from where Tommy sat, not looking directly at him yet.

Staring down at his desk, he took a sip of coffee and winced at its extreme heat. Then he reached under his desk and pulled up his old briefcase, which contained two ties. He opened it and removed one. As he put the tie on, he asked Tommy, simply, "How was your date last night, Tom?"

"It was good, Mark. It was good."

Epilogue

Eva Aguilar confessed to the murder of Sister Margaret and pled guilty in court. The presiding judge sentenced her to finish out her school years at a residential academy for troubled and abused children in Upstate New York. There, she would receive ongoing therapy for the trauma she experienced at Our Lady of Perpetual Hope, followed by ten years of probation. Upon graduation from high school, Eva would continue on to nursing school, becoming a Licensed Practical Nurse and pursuing a long career at the VA Hospital in the Bronx.

Irma Aguilar continued working for the Archdiocese as a janitor but was moved from Our Lady of Perpetual Hope to another Catholic School on the West Side of Manhattan, where she still works today.

Claudia Aguilar also left Our Lady of Perpetual Hope and graduated from Saint Jean's High School. She went on to graduate from Lehman College and became a social worker for the New York City public school system.

Our Lady of Perpetual Hope underwent several investigations and endured years of public scrutiny. It also suffered financially as its student population diminished--a result of both stigma and fear. No evidence of any further wrongdoing was ever uncovered and the school is still in operation.

Benny Hirschle was indeed beaten and did suffer a broken nose during his brief incarceration on Rikers Island. He obtained a lawyer to look at his case for false arrest and imprisonment by the City of New York, however, failed to keep his appointments with his lawyer due to his continued heroin use. Approximately seven months after his release from Rikers Island, Benny was found dead under a set of stairs in a building on East 118th Street, where he had overdosed. His mother refused to identify his remains, and he was buried in the potter's field on Hart Island.

Sharon Stiles continued doing tricks to support her heroin addiction. Approximately six months after Benny returned from Rikers, Sharon was hospitalized for three months after a near-fatal beating from a trick, who raped and sodomized her in their apartment at 155 East 103rd Street. Benny had been waiting on the sidewalk for the date to be over. It was during Sharon's hospitalization that Benny overdosed on 118th Street. Sharon got clean during her hospital stay and moved to a rehab in Westchester County. She has remained sober through the program and currently works at a Starbucks coffeehouse in Mt. Kisko, NY.

Gil Nunez wrote three large pieces about the Sister Margaret case, each one delivering the visceral truth of the story without embellishment or exaggeration, exactly as it was given to him. He has since been given his own weekly column, where he follows in-depth stories on city crime and enjoys a higher salary and quite a bit of notoriety.

All of this, however, is still to come. Right now, we must simply wait for Detective Keane to wake to a new day, and to a new stack of case folders that may become one of our next chapters.

Read on for a sneak peek at the next book in the Tommy Keane series:

HAYDEN JON MARSHALL

Sister Margaret

HAYDEN JON MARSHALL

08:56 am / 1075 Park Avenue, New York, NY

Tommy and Doreen parked and walked up to the complainant's apartment building on Park Avenue, to inquire about the missing earrings. The building was pale cream stone and deep reddish-brown klinker brick, with a hunter green awning. A short black wrought-iron fence surrounded the display of well-manicured shrubberies and ivy that neatly framed the entrance.

The doorman of the building--a tall, good-looking, dark-haired young man with a "bored to death" expression on his face--opened the matching wrought-iron door and greeted them in a sullen tone. He was dressed in a grey wool serge uniform with a grey hat and pristine white gloves.

"Who are you here to see, and who may I ask is calling please?" he said to the detectives, sounding not at all interested in the reply.

"Hey, how ya doing, pal?" Tommy asked, undeterred, "Detectives Keane and Doyle here to see a Mrs. Gillstone in apartment 7A."

He smiled and pulled back his coat to reveal the Detective shield clipped to his belt.

"Okay...I'll have to ask you to go around the corner, please, and use the service entrance. The maintenance person on duty will take you up in the service elevator," the doorman explained.

Tommy looked at him for a couple of seconds. Then asked sincerely, "Excuse me? You want us to do what?"

"I'm sorry, sir, you have to use the service entrance. The main elevator is for residents and their guests only."

"Listen," Tommy began in a low, firm tone. "We may be here to protect and to serve, but we ain't nobody's fucking servants. We're not delivering furniture, or a pizza, and we're certainly not anyone's paid help. Now get this: this Mrs. Gillstone made a complaint, and we are here to interview her and begin an investigation, and if you or her or anyone else thinks we're going to 'go around the corner' and use the service elevator, you're dead fucking wrong. Now hit her bell, announce us, and tell her we're on our way up. You got that?"

"Hey," the doorman seemed to snap out of his trance, "I'm just telling you the rules, man. Believe me, I don't make them; I just gotta do what I'm told."

"I know, and I get it pal. I'm sorry, I'm not looking to give you a hard time. Just tell her we're on our way up, please."

"Yes, sir," the rattled doorman pushed a button on the brass panel on the wall and lifted the handset. In his professional monotone he announced to Mrs. Gillstone that the detectives were on their way up.

Tommy and Doreen walked from the front vestibule into the shiny green marbled hallway. They passed two golden wing chairs and a matching settee on their way to the elevator, which was directly in front of them, waiting with bright white lights and an open door.

"Good job, Tommy," Doreen whispered, amused.

An elevator operator was perched on a stool inside the doors--a short, round man with squinty eyes and rosy cheeks. He had the flushed complexion of a man who keeps a pint of gin, or some blackberry brandy, in his locker to help him through the monotony of an eight- or nine-hour shift.

Day in and day out, month after month, for more than twenty years, he rode the elevator up and down and back up again. Still, he was the jolliest building employee Tommy and Doreen had met so far, and he smiled brightly as they approached the elevator. He was dressed in the same grey uniform and white gloves as the doorman, and he tipped his grey hat to both detectives as they stepped into the elaborate brass and green marble box.

"Good morning! Which floor are you visiting today, please?"

"Seventh, my good man," Tommy replied.

"Yes, sir." The elevator operator pushed the smooth gold "7" on the wall panel as the door closed.

"Look at this," Tommy exclaimed, shaking his head, "these rich fuckers can't even push a button in an elevator themselves. How lazy can someone be?"

"Shhh, Tommy. Let's not get any complaints today, okay?"

"You two on the Job?" the elevator man asked, seeming to relax.

"Yes, sir, we are. Does it show?" Doreen replied.

"It shows. Who you going to see, 7A or 7B?"

"Those are our choices? There are only two units per floor? Wow, they must be pretty nice apartments... A, we're going to 7A," Tommy answered.

"Gillstone," the elevator man said, dropping his cheerful tone. "That woman's a trip. Trust fund kid, bout thirty-five, married to Jarred Gillstone and fuckin loaded," Doyle glanced at Tommy as the operator went on. "He's rarely home. In China now, buying or selling some businesses. That's what he does--buys businesses, fires everyone, then sells em off to foreign countries... And the wife, Erica, she's a nervous wreck busy-body, up everyone's ass all the time, about the most unimportant things. They keep their two kids locked up in some fancy boarding school in Connecticut. Costs more each year than all three of our salaries combined. Let me tell you something, these people may have money, but they got no class."

"Thanks for the insight, pal...We do appreciate it," Tommy replied.

"No problem. My brother's on the job, works in the 66 in Brooklyn. Tommy, Tommy Espana, same last name as me...Either of you know him?"

"No, I don't know that name," Tommy said.

"No, me neither," Doreen replied, "I worked in Brooklyn, but in Housing."

"Housing... Ha, well you're moving on up today, sister! This is no Brooklyn housing project." The elevator man laughed as the door opened to the seventh floor. "The door on the left, folks. Good luck with this one..."

Tommy and Doreen thanked him and exited the elevator, then stood in front of the door marked "A." Tommy knocked lightly and a young Central American woman in a blue uniform answered the door.

"Hello, you are the Police, yes? Here to see Mrs. Gillstone, yes?"

"Yes, and yes." Tommy replied.

"Please, please come in, please… Please wait here one moment please."

She left Tommy and Doreen standing on the burgundy-marbled floor in the entranceway of the apartment. Tommy eyed the foyer and took in the painting hanging on the pure white walls over a small table that held a huge bouquet of fresh flowers. The painting was abstract and muddled with bright colors. 'Money doesn't buy taste,' he thought to himself.

A minute or two passed before the detectives heard high heeled shoes quickly click clacking their way towards them from a distant room. Mrs. Erica Gillstone entered the hall from one of the side corridors, an image of wealth and perfection.

Mrs. Gillstone was a thin and attractive woman, wearing well-fitted black pants and a royal blue silk blouse. Tommy couldn't help but notice her black pumps had matching royal blue soles. She looked magazine-shoot-ready, but both detectives felt she was oddly overdressed for nine in the morning.

"Detectives. How are you this morning? And what took you so long to get here? The Police took my complaint yesterday afternoon. I had expected you to arrive shortly after they left." She barely greeted them as she approached with a black binder in her hand.

Sister Margaret

"Yes, my apologies, Mrs. Gillstone. We got here as soon as we could," Tommy replied.

"Well, this is a very serious matter, Detective... I'm sorry, what is your name, Detective?"

"Keane, ma'am, Detective Keane, and this is Detective Doyle."

"Ah Detective Keane. Well, Detective, this is a very serious matter. You see a pair of very, very valuable, very expensive, and very sentimental earrings has been stolen from me by one of my house staff."

Tommy opened his notebook and began taking notes. "Okay, so how much were these earrings worth, ma'am?"

"At least one hundred and twenty thousand dollars."

"Wow, okay...And you say you know who took them?"

"Yes, Marta. Marta is one of our house staff, here in the apartment. She's fairly new, she's only been with us for about nine months. She's definitely the one who stole my earrings."

"Alright, definitely the one, huh? And how do you know she was the one? Did you see her take them or do you have her on video? Did someone tell you she took them? How, may I ask, do you know it was Marta?"

"Well, I know because she is the only one who would do such a horrible thing. She's young and brash, and sneaky."

"Okay...Other than brash and sneaky, what can you tell me about Miss Marta?"

"Well, she lives in the Bronx. I have her address and phone number in a file I have compiled for you. She is from

Costa Rica and she lives with her sister and her sisters' husband, up there in the Bronx. She is very sneaky, always acting suspicious when she's doing her work around here."

"Okay...And what exactly did Marta do for you, Mrs. Gillstone?"

"She cleaned, did laundry, made the beds. She would run errands when we needed, you know, typical staff things."

"No, actually, I don't know. That's why I'm asking, Mrs. Gillstone. Now, you say you know Marta ran off with your earrings, but other than you *knowing* this, do you have any physical proof that it was indeed Marta who stole your earrings, Mrs. Gillstone?"

"Well...No, nothing physical. But I know it was her. Isn't that enough for you?"

"No, not exactly, ma'am. Let's start here: do you have a photograph, or maybe a receipt, for these earrings? Something we can go on, so we know what we're looking for?"

"Yes, in the file you will find a photo. And you'll also find them on the list of insured valuables I've included."

As Tommy's inquiry went on, Doreen, who was standing quietly just behind him, heard a radio call.

"2-1 Squad, 2-1 Squad, Patrol requesting 85 at John Jay Park for missing child."

"2-1 Squad Central. Copy, en route to location," Doreen responded almost immediately.

"Excuse me, Tommy," Doreen interrupted, "we have a missing child at John Jay Park and patrol is requesting us to 85 them there now."

"Tell them we're on our way," Tommy replied, snapping his notebook closed. "Mrs. Gillstone, we will be in touch. Thank you so much for the file; I'm sure this will help us out tremendously."

"Wait...What? You're leaving? This is a very, very important case, Detective."

"Yes, ma'am, it sure is. But right now we have a missing child that we need to attend to, Mrs. Gillstone, and your earrings are just going to have to wait. You will hear from me soon, but we have to leave right now."

"Are you kidding me?" she raised her voice as Tommy and Doreen exited the apartment door and pushed the button for the elevator. "Detectives!" she shouted again as they entered the elevator.

"Told you. That woman's a trip," Mr. España, the elevator operator, said with a smile once the doors closed.

***

10:12 am / John Jay Park

Keane and Doyle arrived at the entrance to John Jay Park, on Cherokee Place, within minutes. They were approached immediately by Officer Rios, a young and handsome officer of about five-foot-eight with a thin mustache and a determined look on his face.

Rios was one of two uniformed patrol officers who were already on the scene. He stopped Keane and Doyle at the threshold of the park, next to the brick columns and tall black wrought-iron fence, where they had a clear view of the playground to the left, the pool house and East River to the front, and the basketball and handball courts to the right.

"Morning, Detectives. We have a missing three-year-old. The mother over here," he gestured toward the row of benches to the left of the entrance with his radio in his hand, "is Mrs. Marshall. She was sitting on the bench over there while her kid played, and she says she looked up and he just wasn't there anymore. We put out a description over the radio and everyone is looking for him. Sergeant Webber is on his way also," Rios explained to Keane and Doyle, as they each scanned the surroundings.

"Very good. Has anyone left the park since you arrived?" Tommy asked.

"No. No one was really here. We got here just maybe ten minutes ago, if that, and just the few people you see were here. This is the only way in and out, and so far, no one has passed us." Rios opened his memo book and read off the boy's description. "He's a white male, three years old, grey bubble jacket, navy blue pants, grey and blue knit hat, and he was carrying, or last seen with, a brown stuffed bunny."

Tommy's eyes continued to scan the park as he replied. "Great, thanks... Do me a favor, Rios, don't let anyone leave, okay? We're gonna want to talk to everyone here. Hopefully this won't take too long."

Tommy and Doreen approached the visibly shaken woman, who sat on a bench near some large concrete camels in the playground, where Officer Rios had asked her to wait.

"Hello, Miss? I am Detective Keane, and this is my partner, Detective Doyle. We're from the 21st Precinct, and we understand you can't find your son?"

The woman was small and thin, approximately thirty-five years of age. She was dressed well, wearing a black down coat with a fur collar, denim jeans, and what appeared to be expensive tan suede boots.

"Yes. Yes, hello," she said through tears as she looked up at the detectives. "My name, my name is Jessica Marshall," her voice cracked, and got higher, as she continued in a more panicked voice, "and I can't find my son! My son Hayden, my son Hayden... he's only three...Oh my god, oh my god Hayden!" She cried out as she rose to her feet. "He's only three!" she repeated, her entire body shaking in overwhelming fear.

Another woman stepped forward, approximately the same age as Mrs. Marshall. She was short with light brown, very wavy hair, a brown cable-knit sweater with a navy down vest over it, blue denim jeans and sneakers. She was holding the hand of a young girl of about four.

"Hello, Detectives? I called 911 when she noticed her son was missing. My daughter and I were playing on the swings over there, and I noticed her panicking and starting to shout for her son. We looked everywhere for him and when we couldn't find him, I called 911."

"Doreen, can you calm Mrs. Marshall while I speak with Ms. ...?"

"Brownstein," the woman answered.

"Brownstein," Tommy repeated as he turned toward her and walked a few feet away from the other women.

Doreen gently took Mrs. Marshall's arm, and seated her back on the bench, and then she sat close and began to comfort her in low tones.

"What can you tell us, Ms. Brownstein?"

"Nothing really," she replied. "I was at the swings with my daughter, and I noticed this woman looking around frantically, and calling for her son again and again. I pulled my daughter out of the swings and went over and asked her what was wrong. She, she said that she lost her son and I began to help her look. We both called for him, over and over, and we searched the entire park. And then I called 911 and, in maybe two minutes, those officers arrived and then you two came walking into the park. Really, that's about it."

"Do you know this woman? Do you know Ms. Marshall at all?"

"No, I've never seen her before."

"Did you notice anything unusual about her boy?" Tommy asked, and Mrs. Brownstein knitted her brows.

"Actually… Well, I didn't see him at all actually. I was just playing with my daughter when I saw this woman panic and so I tried to help."

"So you didn't see her son?"

"No…no sir, I didn't."

"Okay. Can I ask you to wait a bit in case we have any further questions?"

"Of course, no problem," she replied.

Tommy saw a tall white male, who appeared to be in his seventies, standing with Officer Rios at the park entrance, wearing a long grey herringbone coat with a matching grey scally cap and holding a black wooden cane.

"Hello, sir, I'm Detective Keane from the 21st Precinct. This woman here has lost her son. Did you notice anything unusual, or see the boy at all?"

"I didn't see the boy when I came in a while ago, no. I noticed the mother over there on the bench, by the camels, typing away on her computer, but no, I didn't take notice of her boy at the time."

"Alright. Did you notice anything that seemed unusual to you in the park today? Anything at all, no matter how small it may seem?"

"No, sir, Detective. It's a quiet day. A nice day, pretty warm for November, I think. No one really here. That woman and her son, the other one over there with her daughter... There was an African nanny here a while ago, with two little ones, but she left when I was walking in. Nothing unusual, no suspicious characters, no sir."

"How long have you been here, sir?"

"Oh, I don't know...maybe forty or fifty minutes. I walked in and sat over there, near the FDR, and watched a couple of tug boats pulling some barges up the river for a bit. Came to life and started to look for that boy, when his mother and that nice lady were calling out for him."

"Thank you, sir. Please wait here a bit, in case we have any more questions."

"Sure, sure, anything to help," the old man replied.

Tommy turned and shouted over to Rios who had stepped back towards the park entrance, "Rios, you have his info?"

"Yes, sir," Officer Rios replied.

Returning to the other witness, Tommy asked, "Where did you look, Ms. Brownstein?"

"Everywhere in the park here. And then we all went up to the Avenue as well."

"York Avenue?"

"Yes, that's where I called from. And then I asked this woman--the mother--to come back to the park, while we waited for you... for the Police."

"Good, good. You did the right thing, thank you." Tommy told her and then got on the radio.

"2-1 Squad Central. We have a missing male child, three years of age, last seen in a grey bubble jacket, navy pants, and grey and blue hat, with a brown toy stuffed rabbit, in the vicinity of John Jay Park, 7-7 Street off York Avenue. Please notify all units, and have any available units, plus aviation, assist in an area search."

"10-4, 2-1 squad," came back quickly over the line.

Tommy's heart suddenly started pounding faster as reality hit. A sense of panic and urgency came over him. The thought that they might not find this child right away slipped into his mind, along with a painful fear.

'Where is this boy? Where could he possibly be? How did he just disappear from the park, and how did his mother not notice him walk off or get snatched?' The questions filled his mind in seconds, blurring his thoughts. For a moment he was lost in distress. Then he heard the sound of the police helicopter moving slowly overhead and regained his train of thought.

He walked over to the bench where Doyle and Jessica Marshall were sitting. "Are you currently married, ma'am?" Tommy asked.

"Yes, her husband, David Marshall, is on his way right now," Doreen answered for her.

'So, this won't be an ex-husband, estranged-father kidnapping situation,' Tommy thought to himself. He had almost hoped that would be the answer, they would not only have a solid lead if so, but he felt that the child would somehow be in less danger.

"Listen, Mrs. Marshall, we're going to find your son. We have uniformed officers looking all over the area. Did you notice that helicopter go by just now? They are also looking for Hayden right now. They're checking all the rooftops and alleyways, everywhere we can't see from down here on street level. We'll find him, I promise."

It was a promise Tommy could only hope to keep, but an assurance he felt obliged to give to Mrs. Marshall. Tommy's heart started pounding again, 'God I hope we find this kid,' he thought, knowing all too well that it was not a guarantee.

"What did you do?!" a voice suddenly shouted from behind Tommy's back. "What did you do, you stupid bitch! Where is he? What did you do? How, how? How could you be so stupid! You fucking asshole, where is he? Where is my son? What did you do to our son?" David Marshall stormed into John Jay Park towards his wife.

He stood about five-foot-eight and wore a brown knit cap with knitted geometric designs and ear flaps dangling down the sides of his half-bearded face. His short black down jacket with yellow trim had about a dozen different ski lift passes hanging from the zipper, covering a brown and grey Pendleton flannel shirt, which was untucked and fell over the top of his tan corduroy pants. His skin was flushed red and his deeply furrowed brow was visible beneath his black and orange framed glasses, as he rushed past Tommy towards his sobbing wife.

Just as David approached his wife, Doreen stood up from the bench and put herself between him and Jessica Marshall. At the same time, Tommy reached out and stopped him with a firm hand to the chest, preventing David from getting any closer.

"Slow down, Mr. Marshall," Tommy commanded, in a strong tone. David Marshall slapped at Tommy's hand.

"Take your hands off me! Don't touch me, do not ever touch me," the man cried out as he tried to move around Tommy to get to his wife. "Where is my son? Jessica! What have you done?"

"Relax, Mr. Marshall. We're looking for him now," Tommy began.

"Relax? Who are you, the Police? Well, what are you doing here? Why aren't you looking for him somewhere else? It's obvious he isn't here, isn't it obvious to you he isn't here, Officer?" David Marshall screamed, as he took a step back from Tommy's outstretched arm.

"We have people looking all over the area for your boy, Mr. Marshall. We have helicopters in the sky, and officers everywhere with his description. Now please, sir, relax. We need to ask you some questions."

"Relax? Relax? And what do you need to ask me? Hayden was with that stupid bitch, on the bench over there, she, her, she was the one he was with, not me. She's the one who lost him. Did she tell you anything? Does she know what happened? I bet she knows nothing, does she? I bet the spoiled, princess bitch knows nothing. Do you, bitch?" David Marshall screamed, his face a violent red, as spittle formed at the corners of his mouth. He tried again to move around Tommy, but Tommy stepped forward, and to the side, and stared into Mr. Marshall's face.

"Alright! Enough with the fucking cursing, you. You're gonna relax now, and we're going to ask you some questions. Do you understand me, Mr. Marshall?" Tommy stated, flatly and firmly.

David Marshall looked into Tommy's eyes with a fire of rage, but once he met Tommy's cold, dead stare, he became speechless. The flame of rage was extinguished, as fear and helplessness took over. His eyes went straight to the pavement below and his posture deflated.

"Yes, sir, yes Officer. Of course, of course, forgive me," he said in a low, monotone, voice. "I'm sorry, I know my anger is of no help."

"Alright, it's alright, we understand, Mr. Marshall. This is a very stressful situation. We have several questions to ask you, and Mrs. Marshall. Do you live nearby? Can we take you home and talk to you there? It seems to be getting colder out. Besides, I'm sure Mrs. Marshall would like to leave the stress of the park here. Let's get a little privacy and warm up."

"Yeah, uh, sure. We live just up the Avenue, on 79th Street." David Marshall replied, rather sheepishly.

***

Detective Keane and Detective Doyle walked Mr. and Mrs. Marshall back to their building, 453 East 79th Street, where they had a small, two-bedroom apartment, on the ninth floor of an older brick high rise. They silently entered the building, both Mr. Marshall and Tommy nodded to the doorman, and Doreen guided Mrs. Marshall in. She stared at the floor in a semi-state of shock as they walked along the black carpet runners laid out across the dark red terrazzo floors. The elevator ride was silent.

The four of them entered the apartment and Tommy immediately started taking mental notes. He had wanted to see where they lived. That's why he suggested the apartment, and not the precinct, for the interview.

Not only would the couple feel more comfortable at home, but it would enable Tommy to see where and *how* they lived. This extra glimpse into their home life would enable him to gauge if there were any signs of neglect or abuse, or any other clues that could change the path of the investigation.

They sat in the living area, on a leather living room set that was obviously expensive, but not the least bit comfortable. Jessica curled up in the corner of the couch, as she tried to get as physically and emotionally far from her husband as she could. Tommy and Doreen began by asking them simple questions about Hayden. His age, weight, size and appearance, from his jacket description to what socks and underwear he was wearing that day.

Tommy gave them his cell phone number and asked them to send some photos to him. They asked if there was anything unusual about Hayden--was he shy, outgoing, hyper, or Autistic? Had he ever wandered off before? Was there anyone in the world they would suspect that would want to take Hayden, or hurt their family, in any way?

No answer gave any glimpse of wrongdoing, other than the fact that Jessica Marshall simply had not been paying attention to her son while he played in a public park. On more than one occasion, David Marshall returned to this fact in between questions. "What were you doing, Jessica, shopping on your laptop? Who were you texting that you didn't see him disappear, Jessica? Your Mother? Or maybe your trainer, Jeremy?"

Tommy scanned the apartment carefully: the place was neat and clean. He didn't care for the décor, but there was no crime in having minimalist tastes, uncomfortable furniture, and abstract art on the walls.

"May I see Hayden's room, please?" Tommy asked.

"Of course," David replied. He stood and led the detective to the room, just off the living area. 'A pretty stereotypical, three-year-old's room,' Tommy thought, seeing nothing out of place. The walls were deep blue, and large decals of a dolphin and a beluga whale were placed over an unmade twin bed with sheets that matched the sea life theme. There were stuffed toys strewn about the room, as well as multicolored building blocks and a few large plastic trucks--on the floor, the bed, and the nightstand. Tommy stepped in and carefully looked around, but touched nothing.

David Marshall followed Tommy into the room, and while both were out of sight and earshot of the women in the living room, Tommy stepped closer and spoke softly. "Listen, Mr. Marshall, I know this is a very scary time for you. Please, sir, if I may…please take it easy on your wife."

A glint of rage returned to David Marshall's eyes, but he did not lose his composure. "Yes, Detective, I understand. I know, it's just so…so unnerving." His eyes welled up and a wince overcame his face as he confessed softly to Tommy, "I'm fucking terrified."

"I know you are," Tommy replied, "but we'll find him, I assure you."

"Please, Detective, he's all I have."

The two men went back into the living room, where Detective Doyle was sitting with her arm around Jessica Marshall, who was crying quietly into her hands. Tommy walked over to them, leaned over, and spoke softly.

"We'll find him, Mrs. Marshall. I promise we'll find your son." He placed a hand on her shoulder and then straightened up.

"We're going to leave you now. I think we have enough information, for the moment. Please contact us immediately if you think of anything, no matter how small--anything that you believe may be of interest to us. You have my card and my cell number. Please do not hesitate, any time of the day or night, if you think of something. Please call me."

The Marshalls both thanked the detectives as they left the apartment.

***

Tommy and Doreen rode the elevator down and Doreen asked, simply, "What do you think, Tommy?"

"Fuck if I know, kid."

"He's an intense guy...You think she's going to be okay with him?"

"He's terrified, out of his mind with fear. So is she...This is the kind of thing that kills marriages. If we find this boy or not, this is the kind of thing that can rip a family apart."

"You don't think we'll find him?"

"God, I hope so. Do you remember what they told you in the Academy about abductions, Doreen?"

"What… The Eighty Percent Rule?"

"Yup, eighty percent. Eighty percent of people who are abducted are dead within the first three hours. And Hayden Marshall has now been missing for almost half that time."

"God… I don't even want to think about it."

"Well, it's our job to think about it, Doreen. Let's see what we can do to find this boy, and let's hope when we do, he's still alive."

Travis Myers & Natasha Myers Marsiguerra

Sister Margaret

About the Authors

Travis Myers and Natasha Myers Marsiguerra are a brother and sister team who both grew up in New York City.

Travis is a retired New York City Police Detective, and Natasha works for the IBEW (International Brotherhood of Electrical Workers) Local 234 in California.

Together they form a perfect team in that Travis, who has more stories to tell than a pub full of Irishman, suffers from dyslexia and abhors anything to do with reading or writing. Natasha, his beloved little sister, is an avid reader of absolutely anything that is put in front of her and has been blessed with the gift of gab. She can out-story just about anyone, in any room, at any given time, and she can also type 60 words per minute. More importantly, Natasha is able to understand where her older brother is coming from, and craft his stories into a readable format.

Together, they weave the Tommy Keane Detective series into well-braided fictional tales that are nearly all based in actual events that they, and their friends and relatives, have lived. Travis and Natasha deliver on their promise to tell gritty, honest stories that are rooted in the everyday lives of everyday people.

CPSIA information can be obtained
at www.ICGtesting.com
Printed in the USA
FSHW010824180320
68235FS